Penelope and Adelina

Virginia Gay was born in Ghana in 1951. She studied history at The University of East Anglia and The Johns Hopkins University. She is married and lives in Norfolk.

Penelope
and
Adelina

Virginia Gay

PICADOR

For Brent,
with love

First published 1992 by Sinclair-Stevenson Limited

This edition published 1995 by Picador
an imprint of Macmillan Publishers Limited
Cavaye Place, London SW10 9PG
and Basingstoke

Associated companies throughout the world

ISBN 0 330 32781 X

1 3 5 7 9 8 6 4 2

A CIP catalogue record for this book is available from
the British Library

Typeset by Phoenix Photosetting, Chatham, Kent
Printed and bound in Great Britain by
Cox & Wyman Ltd, Reading, Berkshire

PART ONE

Steaming to Smyrna

JUST AS ADELINA inherited her green eyes I have inherited this diary of her journey to Constantinople. I have her portrait beside me now. Undoubtedly it is the one painted by that monstrous Dickie, judging by the veiled bonnet, the pale hands which definitely belong beside the Shalimar, and the rosewood writing box – the <u>paraphernalia</u> which women like Adelina carry about with them. Her eyes are the colour of honey from bees gorged on clover. Her eyebrows are dark circumflexes. Her shirt is high-necked and stiff, a severe shirt for all its neatly pressed tucks and tiny pearl buttons.

I see that I've lapsed into the present tense but Adelina is dead as a doornail. She died in 1959 and I should know because I am her great-grandaughter. The thing is though, nobody like her could possibly <u>be</u> in the present tense. The conditions in which she existed (I am tempted to write *flourished*) don't prevail anymore. In any case, although she grew dashing and energetic in later life, Adelina's early days were circumscribed and lady-like, those of the perfect professor's daughter.

I have a portrait of my great-great-grandfather too, James Louis Mackintosh, Adelina's famous Papa. He had eyes of Aberdeen granite and a beard which he trimmed with a pair of silver scissors. In another life, not anybody's papa, he was a leading light of Cambridge in the eighties and nineties. He believed in the theory of the aether and was acquainted with the entire Darwin family. I shall not explain the theory of the aether just now though because I would need to consult my former husband, Sam, and that is something which I am not about to do just at present.

I do know one or two other things about James Louis. In the first place, he was the son of a railwayman, an engineer, who married himself above his station to a daughter of the manse by the name of Beatrix. In the second place, James Louis married his housekeeper and kept it a secret for many, many years. Even Adelina did not know until she was quite old, as you will see. Nowadays, people do very occasionally pretend that they are married when they are nothing of the sort, the opposite is far more rare.

As you might expect, I'm much more intrigued by James Louis in all his gravelly dignity than by Adelina, his only child. He remains a mysterious figure whereas I remember her quite plainly, an old lady of ninety whose skin was the colour of faded golden roses and who smelled sweetly of Floris's hyacinth soap. Adelina, my great-grandmother, believed that old people stank, and that if you did not want to stink as well then you had to take drastic steps. Still, an inheritance is an inheritance and I'd better get on with it. It's faintly possible that this diary might turn out another *Edwardian Country Lady*, or even more delightful still, like the papers of that extraordinary lady from Norwich who collected butterflies while at the same time seducing delightfully saturnine foreign gentlemen.

I don't think for a moment that Granny would ever have read a word of this notebook (notebooks really — there are three of them, all bought in Paris in the Rue du Havre and marked 'petit journalier'). I shouldn't think that she knew of their existence. My grandmother, who was born in the Balkan town of Turno-Severin in mysterious circumstances in 1895, did not believe in dwelling on the past. It was the material world which absorbed Granny, money and genealogy especially. She would peruse the *Financial Times* every morning, shaking the pink pages and keeping her eye out for the decanter of ruby red madeira which always stood at her elbow. Granny, it must be said, had no time for Adelina. At the very sound of Adelina's name her blue eyes would turn mutinous and blank. "That woman, calls herself my mother," she would snort as she carried me off to Madame Tussaud's in order to view the waxen Mary Queen of Scots or perhaps the grave young Queen Victoria, more exemplary women than Adelina, in her opinion.

In any case, here it is – the story of Adelina's journey to Constantinople.

*

Hotel Oriental, Marseilles. Saturday August 11th, 1894.

It is not absolutely necessary to have a husband but I have got one all the same. He is taking me to Constantinople. Tonight we will be steaming through the Mediterranean in the direction of Asia Minor. My husband Rupert goes in pursuit of a fortune owed to the firm of Renishaw and Vignier without which we will all be bankrupt. It is not Rupert's fault that Renishaw and Vignier is about to go bankrupt. He cannot be blamed. It is all to do with the money which old Mr. Renishaw put up for the Ottoman loan. Now Rupert wants it back and that is why we are making this journey. As for me, I am going because Rupert is anxious to cure me of the gloomy spirits which have afflicted me just lately. These low spirits, in my own opinion, are owing to discontent rather than gloom, not quite the same thing as any sensible person would tell you. But then Rupert is not entirely sensible, a fact which I do hope to dramatize in this diary of my travels.

Of our fellow passengers, only Mrs. Seawright is an inveterate traveller of the sort who goes journeying in quest of enlightenment as well as adventure. She is to visit the fabled ruins of Asia Minor, the Temple of Diana and the plains of Troy. Mrs. Seawright is an American, a pioneer. She has journeyed across the Great Plains by Conestoga wagon and is not in the least subdued at the thought of falling into the hands of the heathen Turks. She has had two husbands, both of whom were very rich and both of whom are now quite dead, one having died of apoplexy, the other of typhoid fever. The latest of Mrs. Seawright's husbands was a Chicago meat packer but last night when she was reminiscing in the glimmering marble salon of the Hotel Oriental Mrs. Seawright did not mention either of these useful gentlemen but confined herself to speaking of her childhood in the west, where her father was a travelling preacher of hellfire sermons who rode the circuits with a thumping black bible in his saddlebags.

Mrs. Seawright is enormously stout. Her face is threaded with ominous veins and she draws her breath in gulping sighs. I should also add that she drinks a good deal of brandy. Mrs. Seawright is accompanied only by her daughter, who is named Antoinette. This pale lily of a girl she calls 'Nettie'. I cannot describe Nettie with any greater degree of exactitude because she never speaks and I judge people a good deal by what they say. An elucidating word here and there is a great help when it comes to determining character. In addition, Nettie never eats either and it is very helpful to know what people like to eat. I have decided though that Nettie is the daughter of Mrs. Seawright's second husband for her mother must have been quite raddled with age when she was born, more than forty-five, I should think.

At this very moment Mrs. Seawright and Nettie are sitting across the room from me on a sofa of cinnamon-coloured brocade. Their voices are undulating in my direction. Mrs. Seawright is begging Nettie to eat a morsel of croissant.

"Turkish bread is not a patch on this. And you're so pale, just wasting away. You'll get ill and we shan't find a doctor. Only a crumb now."

But Nettie, who is dressed all in white, only shudders theatrically, managing to make her thin and bony shoulders seem substantial and obstinate.

"I can't. Don't make me. Don't even try. I shall be sick if you force me."

There is also a charming Greek family making the journey. Their name is Chrissavelonis. Whenever Madame Chrissavelonis glides into the salon Rupert looks up smiling for Madame is as glossy as Nettie is pale and languid, a crimson rose. From what I overhear, the Chrissavelonis family is bound for Smyrna. As for the rest of the passengers, *they* are not to be found at the glittering Hotel Oriental. I would know if they were because I am very inquisitive and not in the least above asking searching questions or reading baggage labels upside down.

There – I have established myself at the Hotel Oriental. I have presented Mrs. Seawright too. As she is to be a character in my travel diary I am determined to record Mrs. Seawright's story faithfully, as well as my own. For the moment I have left Rupert in the background, a shadowy figure, as the husband of the diarist is apt to be. In any case, I can't write everything down. Some impressions have got to be allowed to fall through my diary net. Mademoiselle Aimée St. Charles, who taught me how to keep a diary in the first place, always maintained that the true delight of diary reading lies indisputably in the fact that the diarist can be relied upon to neglect all the most dramatic moments of her life.

I mention Mademoiselle Aimée because we came down from Paris on the Rapide and at Lyons I was reminded of my old governess because Lyons was her home. Her father was a Captain of Artillery, born at Angers. He had stern eyes and gingery mutton chop whiskers. Mademoiselle Aimée had an unusual grasp of a shapely Latin sentence and this was indubitably why my father employed her. She still writes to me, always in French. I shall write to her, though certainly in English. And to Mrs. Bunn, who is my Papa's devoted housekeeper and Kitty, my dearest friend, and Papa himself too, of course.

Just for the moment though, the atmosphere of the Hotel Oriental being so steamy and soporific (a fine blue haze has collected under the dome of the salon; it is composed in equal parts of eau-de-cologne, Turkish cigarettes and garlic-ridden bouillabaisse), I think that I shall carry on reading my Ouida novel and abandon the notion of writing any more words just at present.

This afternoon we will take a cab to the harbour. Mr. Pullen from the Marseilles office is coming to say goodbye to Rupert. I'm not quite packed yet. There are the gloves I bought in Paris to be stowed away, diaphanous new negligées too.

*

What a lot Mudie's Circulating Library has to answer for. Ouida, I ask you. How transparent Adelina is, already calculating the means of enlivening her days with Rupert. The impatience and ennui rise from her pages like a thin Fenland mist.

Nevertheless, I'm determined to carry on. Adelina is my project just at the moment. I'm suffering from ennui myself as a matter of fact. I've even gone so far as to think of leaving Crick, Frick and Gerhardie. It is one of the oldest management consultancy firms in the City and I don't know how much longer they can keep going just as they are. Old Mr. Crick has grown very eccentric, he wears his fishing things to the office and is always promising a salmon to Victoria, the loveliest of our secretaries. Just lately Victoria has worn nothing but leather to the office, very appealing to elderly gentlemen. She has long legs and a wide sweet mouth and is just beginning to wonder whether it is prudent to carry on buttering up old Mr. Crick. Our financial director is arranging a management buy-out, he's got five million pounds lined up for it and wants to know whether I am interested. He's a far better bet altogether, as Victoria is quite astute enough to know.

"I haven't any money," I told him.

Our financial director's name is Marcus Monckton-Smith. He expects me to be waspish. His hair is mowed very short so that his head is a mass of tightly jostling curls. Marcus plays squash at lunchtime and is very persistent.

When I said that I had no money Marcus only grinned and ran a hand across his curly head. He is the sort of person who thinks that if you don't have any money it can only be because you don't know quite where to look for it.

"You will have, won't you though, when you sell that hideous house of yours in Cambridge?" Marcus suggested.

Yes, perhaps. Just the same . . .

Marcus has been very attentive since he learned of my house. Last week he took me for oysters at Wheeler's. He's got a wife of his own though, all men do. Her name is Camilla and she is always ringing the office to announce that she has locked herself out of her car or her house. She maddens Victoria.

Now that my mother is dead I have inherited Professor Mackintosh's house, you see. It is Gothic. Many people admire it. It's not on grounds of architecture that I deplore the house. It is because I was never happy there that I dislike it so. I am much happier in my little flat near Highbury Fields. It's nearby a greengrocer's called

Margaret Rose. I don't know anyone in my building except Mrs. Munns, my next-door neighbour, and her cat Reginald. I only know them because I met them one day as Reginald was being taken out to have his nails clipped by a distinguished veterinary surgeon.

"You won't tell anyone about my plans will you, Penelope? All very hush hush, you know."

Marcus is always anxious to keep everything a secret.

"Of course I shan't. I'm very discreet."

And I am, in my way.

These notebooks arrived just in time. Where they came from, I shall explain later on.

*

9.00 p.m.

As the wooden shutters were drawn all over the city for the afternoon siesta we descended on the quayside. There the atmosphere was not in the least somnolent. The harbour was a jumble of steam packets. The air smelled of glistening Mediterranean fish and olive oil. There was a southern breeze, sweet and warm.

"We travel by a steamer of the Messageries Maritimes," said Rupert kindly, though of course I already knew this, had indeed arranged the route, steamers being cheaper and more picturesque than the Orient Express.

"They are clean and good. There will be a stewardess."

Particles of black dust were journeying about, adhering in sticky masses, forming clouds. I could not help thinking of my dear friend Walter Ramage from the Cavendish Laboratory and so regarded the particles not simply as dust but as <u>matter</u>. Mrs. Seawright and Nettie were stepping down from their mouche. Mrs. Seawright was proclaiming aloud from Schliemann's *Ilios*, a very controversial book but immensely popular just the same.

Mrs. Seawright's moon face was lit by a rosy fire, perhaps on account of the poetry of archaeology. She did not appear a bit disturbed by the fate of her baggage. They haul it aboard by means of hemp ropes, a thrilling operation. The ropes grind and squeak. Your luggage trembles in the air. The porters and matelots whistle through their teeth at the sight of it, just to terrify the sillier of their passengers.

Nettie Seawright is one of those delicate girls with protuberant gooseberry eyes and a pale high alabaster forehead, very demure in the schoolroom and afterwards rather wicked. The notable thing about her though is that she is perilously thin, thin enough to snap in two, not a bit like portly Mrs. Seawright.

Just the same, despite the whistling of the matelots, Mrs. Seawright continued with her Schliemann, while Nettie began to examine the throngs of jostling passengers on the quayside. Her face held an expression of sweet injury. What was she searching for? Or even, perhaps – whom?

"Extraordinary woman," declared Rupert, though he is not at all the sort of man to eavesdrop on other people's dinner conversation, not to mention being a spectator of the antics of eccentric ladies.

"Don't you agree, Adelina?"

Mr. Pullen from the Marseilles office came to say good-bye. Mr. Pullen has a glass eye, he is very memorable. Obsequious too, where Rupert is concerned, though rather sharp toward me. Evidently Mr. Pullen is quite unaware of the desperate state of affairs at Renishaw and Vignier. He brought a basket of fruit with him for our journey – a prickly pineapple, melons which shone in the afternoon brightness, plump peaches. I do not think that Rupert detects Mr. Pullen's frailties, how anxious he is to guard his own position, how he pretends to know a great deal about affairs at the Ottoman court but only harrumphs when he is asked a forthright question. Rupert observes none of this however, but only tells me what a splendid chap Pullen is. Rupert always believes the best of everyone, perhaps because things go more serenely if you do.

On the deck of our steamer a tiny balding gentleman in a vanilla ice-coloured jacket was flashing his eyes, gesticulating furiously in the direction of the stevedores who swarmed below.

"Italian," said Rupert disdainfully.

"The dottore," said Mr. Pullen softly. "Signor Arturo Banti." For Mr. Pullen is thoroughly familiar with the comings and goings of the Constantinople steamers.

"A very renowned doctor," said Mr. Pullen. "Famous for his remedies."

Finally, I saw who Miss Seawright was looking for. Very intriguing. A Turkish officer. At least I decided that he was a military gentleman because he was wearing a good deal of brightly coloured braid. At first I could not get a perfect view of him but had to shift myself to Rupert's left-hand side.

Rupert is quite used to this sort of thing. He did not think it in the least mysterious of me. He only squeezed my hand and smiled at Mr. Pullen as if to say: "You see Pullen, we've bored her, I'm afraid."

Rupert has grown used to me by now. He knows that I always find the conversation at the next table more absorbing than the one at my own.

In the end I had a fine view of Miss Seawright's Turkish gentleman. A string of porters hobbled along behind him, runnels of sweat creeping down their backs. He was clearly very worried lest they should drop something. He did not notice Miss Seawright though at the sight of <u>him</u>, so tall and liquid-eyed, she took on an innocent, passive expression rather like a sculpted stone lady at the Louvre. She clutched her white parasol. Did Mrs. Seawright observe this little tableau? I think she did, out of the corner of one eye, very tactfully.

The odd thing was this – he *did* notice me. I smiled at him. I even felt a little frisson, smiling at him. And I experienced a moment of knowledge, as if I knew all that there was to know about him – how he smoked cigars, just like Mr. Rochester, and how he spoke many languages, every one with wit and irony, and how at closer quarters his eyes, so remote and affecting at a distance, would turn out shrewd and intelligent. All this I apprehended at a glance. Then I turned away from him, very sharply too, lest he decipher me as I had deciphered him.

In the old days decks were scrubbed down with sand but the deck of our steamer had not been scrubbed. Rupert, who believes in patent medicines, was fumbling in his valise for a particular brown glass bottle given him by Mr. Pullen, an infallible remedy for sea-sickness. It is not that Rupert is especially prone to mal-de-mer, it is rather that he believes in taking precautions. I, on the other hand, have provided against sea-sickness with a box of dry little Parisian biscuits and lots of bottles of fizzy water.

I felt a slight shuddering from the vicinity of the engine room. Then it became a roar. The steamer shifted balance and began to plough the swell. There was the grinding of the anchor. Black clouds formed once again. In nautical memoirs they say that the steamer *screwed* out of the harbour. I do not know what happened to Miss Seawright. She vanished, Mrs. Seawright and her *Ilios* too. We tilted a little in the direction of the sunset – that first delightful intimation that you are parting company with the shore. From where I stood I could plainly see the wrought-iron balconies of the Hotel Oriental, its glass dome and the murky steam which had gathered over the harbour.

At the thought that I was departing for the mysterious,

perfumed pleasures of the East, I felt a curious shivering along my spine, another frisson.

"Did you know that there were crusaders who left from here, Rupert?"

I did not expect an answer. Rupert does not generally comment upon statements of this variety.

"Were there? Dearest Adelina. Your scented hair all falling down. Such a romantic."

Generally Rupert favours a judicious expression. His eyes are blue and keen and alert, always on the look-out for solid things.

I have never been persuaded that Rupert held with romance, though he did invite me to marry him in a deliciously moist botanical garden which is more than can be said for my dear friend Walter, who proposed to me at Fenner's while a stout fielder was struggling with an unexpected boundary stroke. Walter has the kindest, cleverest eyes in the entire world and he has never married anyone else. It is not because he still loves me though. It is because he never thinks of anything but atoms and cricket.

*

I'm going to confess right away that I've already perused this manuscript. I suspect that Dickie Ricardo too read it attentively for it does show signs of having been studied before. At the end of the last notebook there's even something written in quite another hand altogether. I've selected the more absorbing bits, those which can be relied upon to cast an historical shadow. In keeping with Mademoiselle St. Charles' notions there's quite a lot missing from these pages, rather a lot of questions left unanswered, even a page or two torn out. I'll have to see what I can do about filling in the blank pieces. I'm hampered though by my education because when I was a student of history, a long time ago now, my teachers were of the opinion that no correspondences should be drawn between the people of the present and those of the past.

"Miss Katanowska! You are guilty of empathy!" they would exclaim.

A Hepplewhite chair might yield objective evidence but words were especially suspect. What could a word like 'mother' mean, for example, or indeed 'romance'? Not what we might suppose, you could be sure of that.

Now is the time, therefore, for me to produce a piece of irrefutable evidence about my great-grandmother. Before I began reading her journal I imagined that the salient fact about her was that she was born before Herr Doktor Freud took up residence in Berggasse. But as I go along, I'm beginning to realize that this particular fact is of dubious significance. No, the really crucial thing about Adelina is that she was only 4′ 11″ tall and had special hangers in her wardrobe, just so that she could reach her own clothes. The people of the past were neither obtuse nor insensitive. On the whole, however, they *were* smaller than we are. There's all sorts of evidence for this. You don't have to dig up skeletons and subject them to laboratory analysis. You can visit a museum of costume instead. Or observe the short fat doorways and lowering ceilings of English cottages, the fisherman's cottage in Wells perhaps, where my former husband Sam Rewolinski now lives.

And then there's this too: the people of the past were scourged by toothache. By the time that she was fifty (only a fraction more than half way through her life) Adelina's teeth were yellow and rickety. She wore an elaborate plate of ivory, ingeniously constructed for her by a notorious Parisian dentist. She had throbbing, rasping toothache all the time, whereas I never do. There's a mention of headaches too, but we all suffer from headaches, even nowadays.

But look at this. See how we both underline our words, just like Queen Victoria. There's a correspondence for you. A coincidence, I expect.

*

Sunday 12th. An account of my morning.

An unexpected character for my travel diary:

"Addie! My dear old thing! If you're going to do nothing but keep notebooks all day and be a bluestocking, shouldn't you have remained at home with your celebrated Papa?"

As it happens, this morning I was reading Vicomte René Vigier's account of a Parisian at Constantinople as well as keeping all my notebooks up-to-date. While quarantined on his steamer in the Bosphorus, the Vicomte caught a glimpse of another vessel – a Russian ironclad engaged in the transportation of Nihilist women into Oriental exile. This moonlit vision caught the Vicomte's fancy, causing him to remark that in this world there is nothing to be found but mystery and romance. Not quite what I have discovered, I must say.

"Come along now, Addie. Put down that moth-eaten old Vicomte and attend to me."

The voice belonged to someone called Dickie Ricardo. Dickie is a very questionable character indeed. Mystery and romance are not entirely unknown to him, I am afraid. He is apt to pass his vacations in Tangier, Persia and Asia Minor. There are three other things to be known about Dickie. In the first place, he is waiting for his great-aunt Lady Fanny Addiscombe to die and leave him a large fortune. This is his main occupation. In the second place, he is tall and rather spindly, fond of wearing pale straw hats, an aesthete. In the third . . . Well, in the third place, Rupert is not nearly so fond of Dickie as I am, for

Dickie has a habit of always going where someone else can be depended upon to cough up. Until just lately, Rupert was especially good at coughing up. "L'addition, s'il vous plaît," "Die rechnung bitte" and now even "Kach Ghrûsh?" are the only words that he knows in any foreign language.

Dickie is apt to turn up in unexpected places. Once I met him at the British Museum, quite by accident, both of us having decided on a visit to the little Greek temple. On another occasion we met at Crewe station, I was travelling south while Dickie was journeying north for the shooting.

I carried on reading, unfolded maps fluttering about me, bottles of ink arranged haphazardly at my feet: violet ink for my private diary; navy blue ink for my travel diary. When I was a girl, I used to write sensational novels in tall Boots diaries and for that I used to use ruby red ink. That's all over now though. I do not make things up anymore; I am quite grown-up.

There was a veiled bonnet on my knee as well; a postcard from Marseilles for my friend and sister-in-law, Kitty (once known to me as Kitty Renishaw); *Murray's Handbook*; a copy of Clough's *Amours de Voyage*; a bathtub stained Baedeker, all in German, which I read very badly, as well as the Vicomte's account of his excursion to Constantinople.

At the sight of *Amours de Voyage*, Dickie's face lit up. Love is one of his favourite subjects. For other people Dickie recommends the sad, sweet, unconsummated variety, nights without sleep and pale, glistening complexions. For himself he prefers something jollier. He says that this is because he has no talent for romantic literature so that the sufferings of unfulfilled love are wasted upon him.

When I was perfectly calm, I said: "It's always been my ambition to be a travelling bluestocking, but there's already one on board and she's even older than I am."

"Ah!"

I could not help remembering that dear Kitty had once advised me against men who say 'Ah'. Kitty was one of those girls who begins observing the gentlemen at a very young age. I mentioned this to Dickie.

Dickie smiled. He breathed in noisily, dramatizing his dislike of sea breezes, even light, mild ones. He patted my knees affectionately. I wonder what other knees he has patted lately. Am I in good company?

Soon Dickie drew a ramshackle little deck chair near to my own and we began to exchange vital intelligence. Dickie and I have known each other since he was an undergraduate and I was in the schoolroom. He went down from Cambridge without a degree, a disappointment to my Papa and to Mrs. Bunn as well, not to mention Lady Fanny. We are not friends exactly, more of a conspiracy.

Dickie knew all about the Turkish officer who is, it appears, not an officer at all, but a civil servant on his way from Heidelberg to Constantinople (though Dickie, with his relish for the melodramatic, did not say Constantinople but **Stamboul**). All that shiny braid misled me, we don't have soldiers in my family, only sailors. It was in Heidelberg, Dickie swears, that Miss Nettie Seawright and he ran across each other, at a recital of chamber music given by the American Consul. Mrs. Seawright herself had told him so, and I do believe this because Dickie is rather clever at squeezing information out of people. He begins with the deployment of polished manners and flattery and ends up knowing all that there is to know about you. He is going to be Private Secretary to our Consul at Pera, a post where such a talent as his will be indispensable. I do not expect that the job will last long though, Dickie's jobs never do.

"Do you think that she will capture him?"

"No, of course not. He does not even notice her."

"How unbearably sad."

"Not in the least. Can you imagine poor Nettie in a harem?"

In a harem! I had not associated my Turkish gentleman with harems. Nor Nettie either, come to that.

"Ho Ho," roared Dickie. "You're very intrigued, aren't you? Shocked. You do make a picture."

"I wasn't brought up to be shocked. My father did not believe in girls who allowed themselves to be shocked."

I always invoke the name of my father whenever I am on particularly marshy ground. I suspect that Dickie knows this, though perhaps he does not. It is always dangerous to suppose that other people know what you are thinking.

Just the same, a muscle flickered to the right-hand side of Dickie's thin fastidious mouth. I was about to speak but he hurried onward, not allowing me a murmur. Dickie knows things about my father which I do not. I wonder what they are?

"That terrible house! That dragon of a Mrs. Bunn! Antimacassars! What a funny name it is, Mrs. Bunn. It does make her sound splendidly apple-cheeked, don't you think so, Addie? Still, there's more to her than meets the eye, wouldn't you say? I've always suspected the trim line of her ankles."

I said nothing at all. I have never been in the least fond of Mrs. Bunn, you see, and I have never given her ankles the slightest consideration. Papa holds her in very great favour and affection though, there's no use forgetting that.

"Do you remember her scent, Addie? Pungent as moth-balls, don't you agree?"

Dickie sounded for all the world as though Mrs. Bunn were a detestably smelly old lady got up in black bombazine, which she is not. Mrs. Bunn is Papa's house-keeper, the widow of a high class provision merchant from Edgware and a very striking lady indeed, with a sharp nose, brilliant eyes and powdery cheeks.

"Has Mrs. Bunn got a name, do you know?"

"Yes, of course she does. It's Jane Eloise."

"And there's that disgusting seedcake too. Ah, Addie, how I remember the seedcake at your house."

"Tell me, Dickie. Did you know that Rupert and I would be on board this steamer?"

I could see that Dickie was not inclined to answer my question. By now he was in full flight.

"That seedcake. How it crumbled. Quite *dusty*, you know."

But this was going too far. Dickie had been one of Mrs. Bunn's favourites. And the seedcake was always meant especially for Dickie because once he had praised it so extravagantly – "Dear Mrs. Bunn. So delicious. Heavenly. My great-aunt Fanny gives me seedcake. She learned in Delhi, from a Punjabi cook. *Not* so fine as yours."

Deep down inside Dickie is rather horrid, I learned that a long time ago.

As the air grew balmier, Dickie brought out his watercolours and made my portrait.

"Now, Addie. There's a good girl. Compose yourself. Lend yourself to my picture."

"Do I have to?"

"Of course. You must look sad. It won't be too difficult."

His brush flashed away. He was smiling grimly.

"Can I return to the Vicomte?"

"Definitely not."

Dickie is always very grave whenever he is embroiled. The thing is though, he is not tenacious. Within a moment he is generally to be found being grave about something else entirely.

"Shall I look now?"

"You won't admire my work. And I do prefer to be admired, you know, Addie."

He painted all the lines and the hollows which have begun to appear in my face. Up to a point, Dickie believes in the truth. He made me look like someone who smiles a great deal but who also frowns when they think. He painted my hair smooth and brown, drawn back from my face in a distinctly eighteen-fortyish sort of way, perhaps because this was how it was when I first knew Dickie.

I cannot help but feel that he failed with my eyes. Dickie's watercolour showed them practically brown which piqued me rather. They are not brown at all. They are hazel. They have deep watery lights, Mr. Ramage has told me so and he is especially fond of my eyes. I inherited them from my Mama.

"What about my eyes?" I enquired sternly. "They are my only distinction after all."

"Don't be vain, Addie," he replied. "And anyway it's my portrait. *You* are incidental."

At this I lost no time in returning to the Vicomte. Reading is one of my many failings, a very useful escape from being incidental. Perhaps it is worse than a failing, a positive ailment. I have even begun to lie about it so that when Rupert says: "And how did you pass your afternoon, my dearest?" I reply that I went to Whiteley's in order to buy a new pair of gloves when really I pulled my old maroon-coloured chaise-longue into the bay window and spent the entire afternoon reading *Madame Bovary*.

When I told Rupert that Dickie was present on board our steamer he only said: "So that blighter's turned up again, has he?"

*

Adelina does have a grave propensity to ramble on. Memory is especially apt to divert her. I've noticed that. And in their diaries people never do tell you things exactly – what they ate or when they ate it for example. If you investigate you'll find that that's perfectly true. It also explains why it's such a pleasure to read Parson Woodforde because he does tell you those things, and in ferocious detail too. I like to know about the weather, the price of a new ball gown and what sort of flowers were growing in the garden.

Before I allow Adelina to say 'after lunch' therefore, I shall interpose one or two small details. On board the steamers of the Messageries Maritimes lunch was served at ten o'clock in the morning. The food was generally considered to be both insufficient and rather extravagant in the use of olive oil. There was not another bite to eat until six o'clock in the evening.

*

Sunday evening. Out to sea beyond Corsica and Sardinia.

After lunch a fierce squall blew up. Only Mrs. Seawright and I remained on deck, drinking soda water together, soda water being what my stewardess, the frosty Angelina, has recommended to me.

Not that Mrs. Seawright showed any sign of mal-de-mer. As it turned out though, she *was* in the mood for revelations.

Mrs. Seawright was wearing her sapphire blue turban (I had had occasion to observe this garment previously in Marseilles). It was very Byronical and became her wonderfully. She was engaged in drawing up lists of provisions for her trek to the plain of Troy.

"Mosquito nets," she muttered. "Camp beds and a tent. A canvas basin. Our dragoman is a Greek, Mr. Calvert does say that they're much the best."

In an attempt at polite and familial conversation, I enquired whether Nettie was the child of Mrs. Seawright's second marriage. I like to measure my assumptions, you see. It is no good simply <u>imagining</u> that a thing is so. At least, you must imagine first, verify afterwards.

Mrs. Seawright's eyes are the colour of Amontillado sherry and disarmingly candid.

"Oh no. Definitely not. Nettie is the child of my stepson's tutor."

I was rather taken with this disclosure. I sat very still, bristling with curiosity. Mrs. Seawright's face was not in the least softened by this tender memory.

"You see, my second husband very seldom . . . Not like my first, I assure you. He was far more energetic. Of course it was my second husband who loved me, you know. In a platonic sort of way. My first husband, although he liked to . . . had no time for me at all. And there were other ladies of course, lots of them, far more alluring than I am. I never was beautiful, as I expect you can tell. The first married me for my high-spirited ways, the second for my money. It was afterwards that he grew to be fond of me. The tutor was a young German. From Baden. I think that he was called Otto. On the other hand, he might have been named Leopold. I've forgotten."

It is not the sort of detail which I would have forgotten. I've heard that in Paris it is quite usual to be seduced in a hansom cab while bowling through the Bois de Boulogne. I do not know what happens in Chicago. If I am nice to her Mrs. Seawright might tell me one day.

"He was very sweet. Afternoons were always the most delightful time. You can drink tea afterwards. I did not drink quite so much brandy in those days."

At the thought of Mrs. Seawright's dangerous past I was quite overcome with what I can only describe as <u>envy</u>. I think that Mrs. Seawright knew this because she smiled proudly, enjoying my envy, as people usually do.

"And I have brought Nettie to the Levant in order to

escape another romantic entanglement. In her case though, I am afraid it would have ended in marriage."

I imagined a tutor of French perhaps, witty and importunate, perfectly sérieux as well. Or perhaps a dark-haired young man first glimpsed from a box at the opera. With Nettie there is no knowing. She is such a silent girl.

"He is a very worthy young man, the heir to a railroad fortune. With a fine acreage on the Hudson River."

A moment or two passed by. Mrs. Seawright inspected my folding panorama. Was she going to say any more?

I think that Mrs. Seawright sensed my overpowering curiosity.

"It was the experience of my second husband which decided me against the marriage. There are some men who are far too dull to be married to a girl like Nettie. She is fond of romantic fiction, I am afraid. I would not like her to be disappointed. In any case, at Nettie's age there ought to be someone rather more *susceptible*. More thrilling too. As I expect you would agree."

Naturally I agreed. Of course I did. Just the same . . .

"And as to Mr. Murat Bey?"

I mentioned his name hesitantly. You can never know how much a mother has observed of her daughter's behaviour. Some mothers see everything, others nothing at all.

Mrs. Seawright was very crisp.

"Mr. Murat Bey is quite out of the question. Mr. Murat Bey is a foreigner. A Moslem too. Most men are selfish and disparaging in their dealings with women. All the same, there's no need to make a religion of it, is there?"

Next, Mrs. Seawright showed me a portrait photograph of the dragoman who is to meet her at Smyrna. The dragoman's name is Mr. Demetri Nicolopulo. He has the features of an Italian tenor, melancholy and definitely *susceptible*. He is a distinguished dragoman, ex-clerk and travelling courier of Messrs. Thomas Cook & Son and mentioned in all the respectable guide books.

I traced the outline of his beard with my fingertip.

"What a nice face. What a nice man he must be. Does he speak perfect English?"

"Quite perfect. He is writing a book. All the best guides write their own books, you know."

Already stout horses have been engaged for Mrs. Seawright; Mr. Calvert, the American consul, is awaiting her arrival. There is a danger of fever but that is not even to be considered. Salubrious drinking water disposes of fever, Mrs. Seawright claims.

The appurtenances of travel took shape wonderfully before my eyes, horses, couriers and healthy fragrant water. Mr. Calvert has advised a Western saddle which is even now crated in the hold of our steamer. English saddles, in the opinion of Mr. Calvert, are especially treacherous in such rugged territory.

I sat rather shyly, for I have discovered that it is best not to respond too eagerly when you are favoured with untoward confidences.

"There's nothing in it, you realize, this business of Nettie and Mr. Murat Bey. Why, she's never even spoken to him. In Vienna, they tell me, there are doctors who can exorcize *that* sort of thing."

Just the same, Mrs. Seawright's face was mottled with anxiety.

"I could do with a brandy, you know," she said. "Or perhaps something colder. Mineral water is so insipid, don't you agree?"

Then she took up her list once again, asserting her gargantuan will.

"Candles, preserved meats. A lantern."

There is still this to be recorded though: in the evening, just as the old sun was turning the waters of the

Mediterranean to a flood of amber light, I saw Nettie strolling on the deck with Mr. Murat Bey.

I write 'strolling' because she had her parasol with her, a fringed parasol with a shiny silver handle. The waters were calmer now but Nettie was elaborately pale, as if she had dusted her face with rice powder. Her eyes glittered with the tears which she was on the point of shedding. Her fine golden hair was falling in front of her face. Then she darted suddenly nearer to him, tossing back her silky hair. She clutched one of his wrists, the left one, I think it was. She was beseeching him. But Mr. Murat Bey was implacably stern, as if Nettie were nothing but a strange, foreign girl who was behaving extremely badly.

Can Mrs. Seawright be reliably informed? Is there absolutely <u>nothing</u> to this affair?

Poor Nettie. I am beginning to imagine all sorts of fearful, dark things.

*

Fearful dark things indeed. You can expect fearful dark things to happen when you set out for Istanbul with a trunkload of Ouida novels. And it wasn't just Ouida either. Adelina obviously had quite a passion for light-hearted fiction. There are George Sand novels to be found on the shelves of the Cambridge house, Marie Corelli too.

Just the same, it's dreadful to think of, imagine keeping a journal like that when absolutely <u>nothing</u> ever happens to you.

Of course that's often the way. You have to have enormous quantities of time to be able to write in your diary every night. The great trick is to have time for writing as well as an eventful life to write about. I'm not that sort of female at all. I'm an expert in management. I <u>do</u> things. I wear navy blue suits. I'm always rushing about –

tomorrow, for instance, I'm booked on a flight to St. Louis to investigate the acquisition of a chain of insolvent banks.

Not in the least Adelina's sort of occupation. She wouldn't even call it travelling. When she had disposed of old Rupert (or did he dispose of her? I'm not quite sure yet), Adelina walked alone to Lhasa. She wrote books and became a Fellow of the Royal Geographical Society. Adelina did not go to meetings or write reports.

I shan't say anything on the subject of Rupert because I know practically nothing at all about him. He's steeped in mystery. I'd never heard of him until I began reading these notebooks of Adelina's. The business of the Ottoman loan is curious though and I think I shall look into that.

*

Monday the 13th. Stromboli and the Ionian Sea.

In French they say that the sea 'moutons'; the Vicomte Vigier employs this very word in his book. At first it puzzled me but now I think that it must denote the white caps of the ocean, milling and gambolling like sheep in a Suffolk field.

This morning, as the sea was moutonning all about us, Madame Chrissavelonis spoke to me. She said, "Your poor husband is souffrant, Madame?"

I know that Madame Chrissavelonis has noticed Rupert smiling at her, following her movements across the salon of the Hotel Oriental. She is so beautiful that she expects men to notice her and of course they do.

"No," I replied. "He has rather a strong stomach actually. He is occupied with his affairs."

And so he is – Mr. Pullen's report as to how to approach the Grand Vizier, a file of crinkling old letters from the London office telling how Renishaw and Vignier first did business in Constantinople after the end of the war with Napoleon, how they dealt in corn and other matters. Just the same, what I told Madame was not entirely true. Rupert does suffer from chronic indigestion, after all.

Madame Chrissavelonis was far too kindly and discreet to question me further. She smiled and went away with her two little girls to play a round of deck quoits, the picture of a happy woman. Madame Chrissavelonis has exquisite clothes, stitched in Paris. Her name is Mariora and she laughed with her little girls just as if she were nothing but a girl herself. Mariora, Mariora, what a musical name it is. When I was a girl and used to write stories, I would have stolen her name and given it to one of my heroines.

In the wake of Madame and the two little girls there trailed Miss Flora McPhee, an altogether grimmer creature, who is nanny to the girls. Miss McPhee smells of coal tar soap and demands grammatical English and well-scrubbed hands. Meanwhile, Mr. Chrissavelonis has been complaining bitterly of the provisions aboard the *Tigre*. He has promised that when we reach Piraeus he will send for all sorts of delicious treats – caviar and dolmades. I have decided that the Chrissavelonis are perfect in every way and that I shall never write anything bad about them.

It occurs to me now that when I am old I should book passage on a Mediterranean freighter and sit on deck composing my memoirs. I shall write about my mama with her hazel eyes and her three tall sailor brothers, the eldest of whom was named Edgar, while the younger ones were twins who were called Wilfred and Alfred. They were great Anglo-Saxon enthusiasts in my mother's family. I only met my maternal grandfather once and that was when he came one summer to visit Ely Cathedral.

I think now that Edgar, who was my mother's favourite brother, must have fallen in love with Mademoiselle

Aimée. She was quick-witted and fond of poetry while Edgar was tall and slender with jet black hair. They used to go walking in the college gardens together, murmuring in soft voices while I loitered behind on my bicycle. Once too we met by accident at Liverpool Street Station. Uncle Edgar took us roller skating at Olympia and to tea at the Great Eastern Hotel. But can this meeting have been nothing but a sweet accident?

In any case, life is filled with sadness and disappointment. Uncle Edgar retreated to the China coast where he was employed by one of the great trading lines of the Orient while Mademoiselle is the directrice of a young ladies' academy at Lyons, as I have already related. Mademoiselle is in robust health but Uncle Edgar died of smallpox quite a long time ago now. Still, I am not persuaded that either of them would have had the energy for a strenuous life of passion, especially not in a sultry climate like that of the China coast.

*

I've become a detective, stitching together the snippets of the past which do remain. In a wardrobe of that horrid house in Cambridge I've discovered several volumes of photographs. Pale coffee-coloured faces; still lashless eyes; ramrod backs and elaborate stage sets composed of stuffed seagulls and exotic Pacific shells, symbolic of a Scarborough treat. And then I wonder: "Who *was* this and *when* were they?" The mystery of the past to which there is no reply, for the thick cardboard photographs, transposed from fragile glass negatives, are usually quite anonymous. They even smell of the past, a forgotten breath of mignonette mingled with acid coal dust.

My own mother, who followed gentler pursuits than either Granny or Adelina, used to purchase anonymous albums of photographs at school fêtes and market stalls.

She was quite unaware that a dozen such volumes were lurking in a mahogany wardrobe at home. By then, I expect, she had finally learned never to ask personal questions, both Granny and Adelina having done things of which they had cause to be ashamed.

I'm selling that house and I don't mind what sort of person buys it. I've always hated it. There are definitely ghosts there, the fireplaces smoke and the electricity is lethally old so that the ancient fuses are forever fizzing and blowing. But I've taken the fat albums back to my flat nearby Highbury Fields. I've perused them with a magnifying glass and I've discovered one of Edgar and Aimée, Adelina too. Who took it? I don't know. Adelina's mother, I suspect. The girl from the family of jolly sailors who made the mistake of marrying a man who was mostly absorbed in electromagnetic forces. Adelina must have inherited her talent for observation from someone, after all.

I know that the photograph is of Edgar because of his uniform. With my detective's magnifying glass I have examined the double row of brass buttons on his uniform jacket, the braiding at his wrist, the perfectly white peak of his cap. He must have been leaving that very moment. There is a distant manly look to his face though he is very young. He was the employee of a shipping company called Butterfield and Swire, a company which nowadays owns Cathay Pacific.

Edgar is smiling down at Aimée, perfectly besotted in a way which young men can be and old ones very seldom are. Aimée's thick soft hair is parted in the middle and drawn up behind her head; a mass of bright chestnut hair, I happen to know — a colour possessed exclusively by French ladies of a certain elegance. She has dainty wrists, a thick belt with a silver buckle, very narrow-waisted indeed. Only Adelina is cross and plump, leaning against the pony chaise, the hazel eyes of which she was so proud looking cool and rebellious. She is wearing a floppy velvet bow in her hair, white flounces and clumpy boots. The portrait of a very bad-tempered Alice indeed, her black cotton stockings descending into wrinklets at her ankles.

In the background of the photograph there stands that tall icy smoky house, entirely constructed of yellow Fenland brick. The thick walls of the house are inset with windows of pointed arches, even then the conservatory glass was perhaps turning green with damp. After Adelina's mother died in 1879 there were no more visits from the family of sailors at Greenhithe. James Louis was ashamed of his wife's family, the descendants of Thames watermen. A fact which should be borne in mind, it seems to me.

But now it is time to return to the grown-up Adelina, twenty years on. By the light of the famous volcano at Stromboli, she is about to encounter her Turkish Mr. Rochester once again.

*

Midnight.

As we were steaming by Stromboli I met Mr. Murat Bey. He bowed to me as if we were well acquainted with one another. I said: "So you are an archaeologist, Monsieur?"

I spoke in French because that is more polite; it doesn't do to assume that everyone speaks English. Besides, despite studying the vocabulary at the front of my guidebook, I cannot command even a single courteous word of Turkish.

Murat Bey smiled gravely and said that he was not an archaeologist at all but merely a civil servant. He was responsible, he said, for the apprehension of bandits in the province of Smyrna. In the Museum of Antiquities at Constantinople, he explained, I might see the work of a famous Turkish archaeologist but as for himself . . .

Can he really be so modest?

No. Of course not. Handsome people never are modest.

Even so, he was obliged to confess, he *was* an archaeologist. An amateur one. In the longueurs of the Turkish afternoon there are, apparently, oceans of time for *amateurs* of all sorts.

"And are you out to prove that Hissarlik was Troy, Monsieur, or perhaps the very opposite?"

He laughed right out loud, his eyes appearing sharp and bright.

"I am a devoted follower of Herr Schliemann, Madame."

And I expect he is.

Nevertheless, I have been told that Turks are nothing but savages. It is a commonly held belief on board this steamer, even Angelina has warned me, sotto voce. After all, Austria has been doing her utmost to hold the Turks to the Eastern frontiers for centuries. But Mr. Murat Bey is not in the least a savage. There on the deck in sight of the volcano, he began to tell me about the Ottoman Court. The Sultan is called Abdul Hamid and it is only in his reign that the practice of murdering infant princes, nephews to the Sultan, has been abolished. The last Sultan disappeared, no-one knows what has happened to him. The present Sultan spends his days at Yildiz Palace. He lives among splendid shadows, in the clutches of fear. Mr. Murat Bey is, I suspect, a reformer.

"It will be instructive for you especially, Madame, to observe an Empire crumbling."

"For me? Why for me especially, Monsieur?"

But Mr. Murat Bey's eyes only crinkled into a smile, as if I would find out one day. I can tell that he is a tremendous patriot. It embarrasses him to be obliged to account to strangers for his country in this way.

"Shall I see the Sultan?"

"Perhaps. If you go to the Palace for the Friday prayers.

It is called the Selamlik. Would you like that? Shall I take you? It would make me very happy."

I could tell that it <u>would</u> make him happy. He is very definitely the sort of man who likes to make ladies happy. His eyes have a fine quizzical glint. If you allow them, they pierce your soul for you.

"Yes, oh yes. I would dearly like to go. More than anything in the world."

More than anything in the world. What a thing to say.

What a <u>shameless</u> thing to say. But there it is. I did say it. I do not regret it either. Not a particle. My friend Kitty once advised me not to go in for regrets, that they would not become me, and in so far as I can, I always do follow dear Kitty's recommendations.

But before I lay down my pen for the night there's this to add: Not half an hour ago Rupert and I made love together. Is it still love? I have not decided yet. His body seemed very pale and soft compared with that of Mr. Murat Bey. Where once the event was prolonged and sweet it is now accomplished exceedingly quickly, with nothing but a touch and a sigh. Not a breath of words, though. Rupert does not go in for words. I do, however. I recorded it all, in violet ink, scrupulously truthful to the last.

*

What a hideous little addendum. Poor Rupert. It's absolutely the first time I've sympathized with him since he failed to imagine the Crusaders at Marseilles. I can never imagine the Middle Ages either. I can imagine <u>Adelina</u> though, stiff in her bunk, thinking of England as she eagerly waited to get it all down in violet ink. And who needs words at a time like that? I ask you.

But it has just occurred to me that perhaps she wasn't thinking of England at all. Perhaps she was thinking of

Mr. Murat Bey instead. What an intriguing possibility. How disloyal of me even to imagine it.

*

Tuesday the 14th. The Ionian Islands.

This morning I came abruptly face to face with two versions of my character. Here they are:

As I sat before my looking glass clamping down my hair with a silver comb, Rupert came hurrying in. He was searching for one of his shirt studs. They are small and made of mother of pearl, they get lost in no time. Rupert was very cross because he could not find it. His voice struck a vinegary note.

"Haven't you seen it? You must have done. I rely on you to find things for me, Adelina."

"No, oh no. And I can't see into the looking glass with you standing there."

"Well, I've got to have my stud, Adelina. I can't get dressed without it, you know."

I was a little breathless. My hair is thick and heavy, not a bit silky like Nettie Seawright's. It makes you catch your breath, winding your own thick hair around a lump of old stocking then fastening it down with bony sharp pins.

Rupert's fingers caressed my forehead. I did not altogether like it. I thought of asking him to stop.

"You've got a headache, my poor Adelina. There are grey patches beneath your eyes."

Grey patches indeed! And to be called "My Poor Adelina" like that!

"No, I have not," I replied, as crisply as possible.

Rupert prefers gentleness to crispness. His voice assumed a certain timbre, as though I sapped his energies. He spoke very patiently.

'You must always tell me the truth. Especially when it concerns your health."

I said that I was always <u>exceedingly</u> truthful and that I was distinctly alarmed to find that Rupert had not realized it by now. I believe I added that our sea voyage was doing me a world of good and that I had been immensely cheerful since we left the port of Marseilles and had had hardly any headaches worth mentioning.

I think now that I must have spoken with too much asperity. Rupert does not entirely believe in my headaches, you see. He grew a little rosier. There was even a muscle twitching in his cheek. I could see him in my looking glass, deciding whether it would be a good idea to lose his temper. In the end he exploded:

"My dearest you are growing neurasthenic. I had hoped that we . . . that this visit . . . If only you could learn to take life a little more calmly."

Rupert was lost for words. It has taken me a long time to understand that he does not require me to be <u>cheerful</u> so much as <u>calm</u>.

I, on the other hand, had rather a lot to say. I could feel that there were thick veins pulsating in my throat. When I was a girl, Papa arranged for Mlle. Aimée to accompany me to a series of lectures on the circulation of the blood. I did not enjoy these lectures, which soon progressed to lessons in anatomy with a rattly skeleton by the name of Gertrude. I dislike the notion that there are things going on inside my body which I can neither observe nor regulate. Anger, I could not help remembering, was one of those same things.

"I'm not neurasthenic. Though I think you mean hysterical, don't you? And by the way, is this your stud? I think it is."

I threw him the stud. He fielded neatly. Cricket is one of the few things that Rupert and Walter Ramage have in common.

Rupert did once call me hysterical. I do hope that he has lived to regret it.

Now Rupert glared at me, perhaps because he generally means exactly what he does say. That is the advantage of taciturn people. When they do utter, they tend to have considered their words beforehand.

"Hysterical!"

Rupert flapped a bundle of papers under my nose, all with the Renishaw & Vignier imprint at their head, some of them the work of the firm's new typewriter – a long-nosed young lady from Streatham, Miss Watson.

I have allowed myself to entertain doubts on the subject of Miss Watson. These doubts, I am ashamed to say, rather hotted up my anger.

I stood up, took firm hold of my round box of peach-coloured face powder and employed my scented puff in order to dust Rupert down.

"What are you doing? You can't. I say. Stop it right away. And you used to be so gentle. Just look at me."

A cloud of pale sweet dust filled the air. Rupert was covered in it. By the time that I was finished with him he definitely needed a stiff brushing, he was spluttering too.

"Oh, what a cat you are. How could you?"

He was very aggrieved, I could see that. He was doing his best to brush the powder from his cross, pale face.

"I admire cats. And you can find your own studs from now on, Rupert."

Rupert snorted, his long thin face turning from white to violet, his hands twitching with rage.

"You'll murder me. You'll give me a heart attack."

"Perhaps I shall. I'd be careful if I were you. I should take a deep breath and count to a hundred."

After that he vanished rather quickly. I have learned over the years that actions of this kind forestall hours of painful discussion though they are often followed by long stretches of silent recrimination.

I don't think that Rupert <u>would</u> take up with a girl like Miss Watson. It would be undignified. It would be more in keeping for Rupert to keep a jolly blonde mistress in a villa at Epping Forest. That is what his father did, after all.

As for the other version of my character, that must come later because now it is time for our infamous luncheon. Mr. Chrissavelonis is talking about the cavier and dolmades he is going to order when we reach Piraeus. He's a great gourmet. Or do I mean gourmand? He's both, I expect.

*

Look into it I said, as though the business of the past was all there, waiting to be discovered in some celestial library. Instead there are nothing but clues and all sorts of boring loose ends to be followed up. The Guildhall Library, I understand, keeps records of the Stock Exchange, while the Baltic Exchange has its own archivist. There's also an establishment in Kent presided over by a dim old colonel, Marcus has told me. I'm just beginning to wonder if it wouldn't be more efficient simply to make everything up. But unlike Adelina, I have had the benefit of higher education and ought to be able to compare one version of an event with another. I can sift fact from fiction too, fiction being finely shaped and turned while it's really fact which is the loose and baggy monster.

Naturally, this capability is what makes me such a splendid success as a management consultant. I can build up a pretty clear picture of the mistakes which have been made in the past and then proceed to write a lucid account of them. And of course I'm never required to act on my own advice – I move right along to the next assignment. I don't have to get things perfect or suffer the consequences of my own recommendations. I'm an expert in management, after all.

(What is it that I was going to look into? Oh yes, the

Ottoman loan. The Ottoman debt was a constant occasion for anxiety in the last decades of the nineteenth century. The Empire had to be propped up and its debts rescheduled all the time, according to the *Cambridge Modern History*. You've got to have a vast fortune if you're going into the business of underwriting grisly emperors.)

When I went for my first interview at Crick, Frick and Gerhardie they said: "But you don't know anything, do you? You've spent your whole time in libraries, haven't you?"

I explained that when you've learned to read and write and think and listen and write up a lucid version of events then you can learn practically anything in double quick time and that of course you can deploy all these abilities in any theatre at all.

Mr. Frick, who wore a toothbrush moustache of the 1915 variety, remained dubious.

"Well Miss Katanowska, we can't make an offer on the spur of the moment. And I wouldn't read too much into *that* if I were you."

I've moved on since then. Mr. Frick was booted out long ago. His terms were lavish. Now he lives in a delightfully ruined castle nearby Fort William and is an expert on British business. He's a fellow of dozens of institutes. I've become best at answering the question which goes: "How do you see yourself in ten years time?"

I've taught myself to look forward. It's an art. Adelina ought to have learned it sooner.

*

Steaming through Peloponnesian waters.

Whereas Rupert is always insisting that I require tranquillity, Dickie is of the opinion that *adventure* is what I need.

I sat on deck from seven o'clock this morning onwards. I had my folding panorama: I was busy identifying the islands of the Ionian Sea. Dickie wears horrid soft-soled shoes. He can creep up on you.

"Addie, you are the very picture of a disconsolate woman."

"No, Dickie. I'm a very happy one."

Dickie is not at all a sympathetic person so it is much the best never to confide in him. I did not tell him about the peach-coloured powder. Just the same, he did not give up.

"My poor Addie. You are a woman tout à fait sans histoire."

Dickie has a delicious French accent, sibilant and full of undulation. With his nimble tongue he makes 'sans histoire' sound like a lethal wasting disease.

Naturally though, I do not take to being called 'Poor Addie' any better than being called 'Poor Adelina'. Dickie however is not my husband and so I allow him rather a lot of latitude.

"And you really think that I ought to acquire one?"

"Of course I do. For the good of your soul."

I pointed out that all sorts of admirable people had had a dull time of it before going on to more scintillating experiences. I mentioned one or two of them: Florence Nightingale, for example, and Elizabeth Barrett Browning.

"And then there's your great-aunt Lady Fanny, from whom you hope to inherit lots and lots of money. She had an exceedingly tedious life before she acquired her fortune and became interesting."

"There you're wrong. Aunt Fanny has had masses of adventures. Aunt Fanny was in the Indian Mutiny."

"But how could it be my fault that I was not in the Indian Mutiny?"

"Not only that. My great-aunt Fanny had a most

absorbing love affair. With her Professor of Sanskrit, as a matter of fact."

I found this news disarming. I have met Dickie's great-aunt. She struck me as especially unbending, a lady of the tough, stringy sort, like an elderly French bean. The idea that she was once far more lubricious, diverting herself with learned foreign gentlemen, was very disquieting. The thought of Mrs. Seawright and her stepson's tutor, Leopold (or perhaps Otto), sprang immediately to my mind as well.

I could feel the wrinkles deepening upon my brow.

"Now you're looking unhappier still."

"Now look here, Dickie."

"It's true Addie, I swear. She recounted the story to me in every detail. She's not in the least ashamed. He seduced her by showing her his collection of erotic Hindu sculpture."

This conjured up all manner of pictures. The professor murmuring over her, describing the postures of the voracious gods and goddesses, Lady Fanny crisp and unbending at first. Then, as the power of the professor grew, as the afternoons grew more sultry, as the punkah creaked away . . .

I dismissed these disgraceful images instantly. It's one thing to read George Sand, quite another to start making up the stories yourself.

"Do think what you are missing. Mutinies, lovers, adventures of every sort." .

I should not allow Dickie to speak to me like this. He is a dangerous type, it's the only thing that Rupert and Papa agree about. They say that men like Dickie are obliged to consort with every type of low person and that they cannot help it. But I've always found a conversation with Dickie to be curiously soothing. You can say whatever you like to him and the very worst that can happen is that he'll appear rather bored and say that he has a tea party to be going to. Dickie would not dream of shouting at you, or allowing his face to turn purple as stewed plums with rage. Nor does he tell you what a worthless, hopeless person you are. Dickie is of the firm opinion that we are all worthless in our own ways.

"Spot of champagne?" enquired Dickie kindly. "I like a drop in the afternoon, don't you? I shall summon a steward. We'll have a nice drink together."

"Yes," I agreed. I was feeling a little thirsty, what with the erotic Hindu sculpture and so on.

"Dickie?"

"Carry on, dear Addie."

"I was just thinking."

"Think away."

"How old do you think your great-aunt was when she met her Hindu gentleman?"

"Very old indeed, Addie. Withered. Far older than you. In any case . . ."

"Yes?"

"I don't think that a person can ever be entirely too old for that sort of thing, don't you agree?"

*

Aha! So Dickie *was* gay, was he? I suspected that there was something unusual about him even when I was five years old, sitting on his lap in the middle of the sultry Victoriana of Professor Mackintosh's house – Doulton pots and the faint scent of Adelina's Turkish cigarettes. In the bookshelves to the right of the marble mantle were Adelina's works, thick volumes in maroon cloth covers. Delicate sketches of donkeys, butterflies or whirling dervishes adorned their fronts. They were printed by Sampson, Low at Fetter Lane and their titles were dashing ones in the finest tradition of English exploration: *With Pen and Ink in Little Tibet; An Idle Woman at Persepolis.*

In any case I do remember Dickie Ricardo, I'm glad to say, because as things turned out he had quite an influence on me. Adelina introduced us, puffing one of her stubby scented cigarettes.

"Dearest Dickie, this is my great-grandaughter. Her name is Penelope. She is the daughter of a Polish war hero. An impractical man, a coward in private life, but a war hero just the same."

I noticed that there was a black hair growing out of my great-grandmother's chin. I did hope that she was not going to discuss my wayward father in front of Dickie.

"Penelope. What a treasure. You have Adelina's eyes."

He peered at me. It amused him that Adelina should have a great-grandaughter. I was an unexpected benediction. His own eyes were filmy, yellowish.

"There's intelligence there, Addie. She has definitely inherited your eyes. You were so proud of them, do you remember? A suspicion of malice too, I'm delighted to say."

"And my tongue too, Dickie. Do be careful."

Even at that age I noticed that they kept on saying one another's names, Dickie and Addie, just like characters in a crackly play on the old Home Service, as if you might forget the identity of the one who was speaking. Their voices too were a remnant of the past, not like flesh and blood creatures at all. Dickie's was thin and fizzy as sweet mousseux while Adelina's voice, on the other hand, resembled vintage port, deep and prune-coloured, in the manner of a renowned Lady Bracknell saying 'handbag'.

With the scrupulous manners of a very old man, Dickie offered me his hand. It was a very sharp and bony hand, like one of Adelina's vicious hair pins. His fingers were papery dry and chilly. There were rumbling, gurgling noises thrusting up from deep inside him. He wore a knitted waistcoat with a pattern of bright diamonds and a bow tie.

"I can tell that we are going to be the very best of friends, aren't we?"

"That," I replied, "remains to be seen, Mr. Ricardo."

*

Wednesday, August 15th. Piraeus.

Mr. Chrissavelonis has indeed sent to the best hotel in Athens for his provisions, just as he threatened to do. He has been striding about on the quarterdeck, wearing a hat of smooth golden straw and consulting the list which he has been making for the last three days. There are to be hams, eggs, dolmades, sirloin, wine too and raki, all destined for tomorrow night's moonlit dance. From time to time he holds up his two sturdy, dark-haired little girls so that they may catch a glimpse of the Acropolis.

I know now that Mr. Chrissavelonis was brought up in Smyrna, that he was born a citizen of the Ottoman Empire and that he is returning to Smyrna in order to comfort his newly widowed mother. Madame Chrissavelonis, who speaks so many languages, was born not in Smyrna but in Bayswater. Sometimes, now that we are in Greek waters, Mr. Chrissavelonis bends down in order to murmur in Greek to the little girls but I do not think that they understand him. Their Scotch nanny has done her work far too devotedly for that.

But what was I going to describe next? I know, the drama at the luncheon table. It happened like this. Nettie entered, timid behind her cloud of fair hair. Mrs. Seawright, whom I must learn to call Abigail, followed. Then she took Nettie's elbow and led her to the table. (We sit at one table, a long one, with the Captain at one end. Signor Banti, who is the ship's doctor, sits at the other end.) Mrs. Seawright's face was drawn and troubled. She dashed a white hand across her forehead. Like many people who

43

are fat, she has delicate narrow feet and minute pale hands.

Nettie, who is thin as a wand, stumbled on her way. Then, after the two of them had sat down, Mr. Murat Bey came dashing in, a breath of sun-warmed salty air about him, so that I knew he had been seated on deck, his fine eyes (they are the colour of demerara sugar) and hawk-like nose turned upward to the sky.

He nodded in my direciton, then to Rupert, then to Dickie. He did not even blink in Nettie's direction. I think that he was whistling *Florodoro*, as a matter of fact.

Tears began to purl down Nettie's cheeks. She never made a sound. A mute portrait: Whistler's White Girl in a flood of silvery tears. Quite a lot of gentlemen might have melted at the sight of her but Mr. Murat Bey did not quiver.

Neither did Mrs. Seawright. Her stoical expression said: "This is quite usual. Girls do cry, you know."

She did sigh though, and was eventually obliged to grasp Nettie by her narrow lace cuff once again and sweep her out of the saloon.

In the absence of the Seawright ladies we all smiled at one another, relishing the drama. Doctor Banti was especially attentive, following the English conversation as best he could.

A moment or two later Mrs. Seawright returned. Claret-coloured veins stood out in her face. She prepared to wade into a soup plate full of mutton and red haricot beans.

"Frightful muck," pronounced Mr. Chrissavelonis in his quaintly accented English.

"I've given her a pinch of laudanum," declared Mrs. Seawright. "Let us hope that this does not happen again."

"I will mix a special powder for Signorina Nettie," said Doctor Banti.

"Poor young lady," said Madame Chrissavelonis.

All the ladies were very sympathetic. It is not in the least true that women are unkind to one another, especially in matters of unrequited love.

The saloon clock ticked ominously. Mr. Murat Bey, I regret to record, was hunched over his own soup plate rocking with wicked illicit laughter, for Moslems, as is well known, do not take the sorrows of women as gravely as they ought.

Naturally, Mrs. Seawright did not spare him another glance. Mrs. Seawright's two rich husbands have set her above petty matters, Turkish civil servants and flighty girls. Mrs. Seawright is a resolute woman in all circumstances, never discommoded in the least.

"A game of cards this evening, I think. Whist perhaps. Madame Chrissavelonis? Mr. Renishaw?"

Madame Chrissavelonis gave a charming smile. She bowed her head, a tendril of glossy curl escaping as she did so. She appeared quite excited at the thought of a game of cards. Her cheeks were rosy, her velvety eyes glimmered.

"Why yes, Mrs. Seawright. Such a pleasure. Shall we say eight o'clock? Do let us say eight o'clock."

And to my astonishment Rupert too agreed, and with alacrity as well.

*

"Katanowska? You did say Katanowska, didn't you?"

Colonel Hevingham stopped, overflowing with suspicion. He was wearing a misty green Norfolk jacket, as if to remind everyone that this was not a proper job, only being a colonel was a proper job. He has keen and glinting blue eyes which are always looking at a point somewhere a little beyond your head.

He wrote my name down in his notebook.

"You had better give me your address as well. Would

you like some coffee? Not instant, you know. Proper coffee. Ground coffee."

"Yes, please. That would be lovely."

At first Colonel Hevingham's eyes reminded me of Rupert Renishaw's till I remembered that I had never met Rupert, thank God. Rupert was absolutely not my type.

"Is it a Polish name?"

"Mmm."

"And how did you come by it?"

People like Colonel Hevingham do get away with monumental impertinence, I've found. If you ask *them* personal questions they turn distinctly frosty.

"It was my father's."

The Colonel smiled grimly.

"I did run across one or two Poles. That was in Vienna. They were on their way home."

"Unlike the Cossacks and the Yugoslavs. They didn't quite get home, did they?"

"No. No, they didn't."

Colonel Hevingham shivered a little, as if this cutthroat betrayal still chilled his blood. He began to speak of a certain night in 1946 when he had drunk vodka from the Schneider Trophy in Vienna.

"My father stayed in England after the war. He returned to Poland later on."

"Ah."

"My mother was a Wren. She spoke rather good French – she liaised with the exiled delegations."

That was at the end of the war though. At first she was a radio mechanic in naval bell bottoms and a seaman's jersey.

Colonel Hevingham rubbed his hands.

"Very becoming get-up, Wren uniform. Tricorne hats you know. Nice well-cut suits too. Now what did you want, Miss Katanowska? Ah yes. Records of partnership. The Ottoman loan. Let me see . . ."

I did not mention that my father escaped from the Germans by flying to France in a Gypsy Moth. He had three young sisters, the daughters of an indulgent fur merchant. My father was the eldest, an air force cadet. His sisters were named Eugenia, Maria and Katharina and I picture them living on separate floors of a cream-painted Mozartian town house at the heart of Cracow. Eugenia wears gold spectacles and mutters to herself in many languages. Maria wears sophisticated black. She is a player of nocturnes and is only useful ·for standing in grocery queues. Katharina, the little sister, is a fine cook. She sews on buttons and her eyes fill with tears at the least breath of criticism. There they are, a portrait of my unknown aunts. In the absence of any evidence I have allowed them to remain virginal, sisterly and eccentric.

"Now. In the time of Abdul V . . ."

Colonel Hevingham, in addition to his Norfolk jacket, was wearing brown shoes which required polishing. I took this as a sign of failing powers. I could see that he was still deeply embarrassed.

Colonel Hevingham, it's time I explained, is archivist to an exclusive library of finance. This library is to be found in a stately home of Palladian design in East Kent and it is funded by private donations as all our libraries soon will be. If it hadn't been for Marcus, I would never have heard of it. One bracing day a few weeks after Christmas, when the snowdrops and aconites were beginning to flower, I caught a train at London Bridge Station and went to visit the library.

Colonel Hevingham presides over records of ancient opium sales and forgotten panics – there was one in 1893, for example, the year before Rupert and Adelina set out for Constantinople. There is a project to enter the old paper records of the outmoded Stock Exchange into a gigantic Data Bank. And there are paintings too – the walls are lined with portraits of black and white tiled Dutch counting houses and rowdy Suffolk horse sales. A celebration of the marketplace. It is practically impossible for an old Colonel to earn his living.

"Here you are, Miss Katanowska. I've done a real Staff College job for you. All you need to know. The file on Rupert Renishaw."

I find that one mention of Crick, Frick and Gerhardie always gets me the very best of information. Nowadays information is almost as important as money. It's no good telling people that you're interested in genealogy, that your grandmother was born in dubious circumstances in a Rumanian border town and that you're not quite certain who your great-grandfather was. That sort of thing doesn't go down at all. You'll only get treated like tiresome Australians in search of their ancestors, nothing but an impediment to the worthy system of local archives.

So there I was, with the file on Rupert Renishaw.

Quite a narrow one as it emerged.

*

And now, the whist party. I took a sheet of writing paper, a piece of blotting paper and a glass bottle of black ink. The creaking old saloon was redolent of Mr. Murat Bey's cigars. Fortunately, in view of the conversation, this was the only way in which he made his presence known. Here is what I wrote:

8.00 p.m. – The saloon of the steam ship *Tigre*, the climate sultry, our engines chuntering. I am here only to observe, quite out of the picture.

Signor Banti, our ship's doctor, has provided an egg-shaped walnut table for the card party. The table is inlaid with foliage of a paler wood at the points of the compass. I think that it is yew. Mrs. Seawright has tugged at the brass oil lamp so that there is light spluttering not far above them. Mrs. Seawright is grave and concentrating, arrayed in prune-coloured silk. Card games are a serious matter, after all. She is to partner Signor Banti. Rupert, it seems, is to play opposite Madame Chrissavelonis. Does the prospect please him? I think so. The horizontal lines in his forehead have eased a little. All the Renishaws adore games, even my dear Kitty, the most intelligent member of Rupert's family. Backgammon, patience, tennis and croquet golf, they delight in them all. Rupert's unmarried sisters, Lucy, Marie and Letty, still live together in the villa at Blackheath, playing dominoes and snakes and ladders every night. Sometimes Rupert goes to have a game with them. Their cats are allowed to lie on top of the card table purring. The dogs, who are called after generals, lie snoring beneath the card table. Lucy, Marie and Letty adore Rupert though they do not allow him to manage their investments. Love is not blind, in my experience. It is simply love.

Madame C. is wearing her second-best pearls to-night. They glow like rosy milk in the light of the polished oil lamp. Hanging on her wrist is a bracelet of heavy gold. Dickie says that Madame's father is a powerful financier and that Monsieur C. is a cousin of hers, sent for from Smyrna in order to enter the family business and become a malleable son-in-law. Last year, Dickie says, Madame gave a ball at which all the ladies received tiny watches studded with precious stones. Afterwards the society papers wrote that it required more than money and fine presents to make a splendid ball. Dickie says that Madame gave no sign of injury but bore this envious cruelty quite cheerfully and that now everyone is counting their chances of being invited to her next ball.

Signor Banti, respectfully known as 'Dottore', is wearing a velvet smoking jacket, midnight-blue in colour. His eyes are eager, black too, as black as morsels of polished jet. The dottore mixes his own remedies, some of exotic eastern provenance. My stewardess Angelina has a high opinion of him because once he cured her of a ticklish rash on the back of her knuckles. It is plain that the dottore does not know the meaning of the expression 'poker-face'. He pounces on his cards, sometimes lovingly and full of gloating, and at other times with a groaning sigh and bitter smile of resignation. This afternoon the dottore has been ministering to Nettie and he has no shame in describing her condition to the assembled company.

"She eats, Signora, not one speck of food. I have seen young nuns of Siena in her condition. She . . . They . . ."

English fails the dottore. He blusters but he blusters in Italian. He is not acquainted with the sensibilities of American young ladies, he has definitely never perused a novel by Mr. Henry James. At the mere whisper of the word 'nuns' Mrs. Seawright shivers. Despite her poker face I know that the doctor is confirming her deepest fears. Mrs. Seawright, just like Charlotte Bronte, possesses an abiding horror of Roman Catholicism.

Madame Chrissavelonis, décolletée, leans forward. The diamond clips glitter in her lustrous hair. She translates.

"It is not uncommon, you see, for signorinas, young ladies, who suffer in this way to . . ."

Perhaps the doctor had not expected his words to be conveyed after so bald a fashion. There is blood rising in his brown cheeks as I write. The eyes of polished jet are flashing. Still, he is ploughing on, Madame C. leaning forward once again.

Perfectly impassive, Mrs. Seawright is arranging her hand.

"To make things up? I guess that's what you're suggesting, Signor Banti?"

Overflowing with relief the doctor nods. It is a nod of consummate admiration. Mrs. Seawright is so splendidly detached.

"That is so, Signora. A revelazione."

Quite a lot of things sound more dignified when conveyed in a foreign language. I catch Rupert's eye across the saloon. The corners of the saloon are obscure, bathed in shadows. The walnut table and the four faces, Rupert's especially, are gently illuminated. There is an undefended melancholy light in Rupert's eyes to-night, as if in the presence of strangers and foreigners (there are languages in which these two words are the same) he were able to subside into a less disdainful version of himself. I remember how he said "An Italian" at the quayside in Marseilles. Just the same, at the present moment he is absorbed in what the doctor has to say.

Mrs. Seawright, having arranged her cards, now snaps them together tightly.

"Who dealt this hand?" she enquires, stern and deprecating.

*

They were playing for money. In later life Dickie and Adelina always played for money. Without the prospect of money there would have been no thrilling excitement. I can see them now, monstrously old and bright-eyed, gloating over their winnings.

While Granny was dancing, Dickie and Adelina spent the entire Second World War playing cards. They played with soldiers convalescing in the Cambridge colleges. They played at the Stars and Stripes Club. They played while Colonel Hevingham was busy in North Africa and Crete. Adelina once confided to me that Dickie used to cheat, peering myopically at other people's hands while making a quick dash to the gents. In any case, the first notebook of Adelina's journey to the Levant – a 'petit journalier' purchased in the Passage du Havre in Paris – is about to draw to its close. How very like a three-decker novel it all is.

Speaking of three-decker novels though, I have discovered something which is puzzling me. An entire tea chest filled with romantic melodramas. I found them in the attic of the Cambridge house, perilously close to the rusty water tank. The tea chest was nailed up. I was expecting to find a guilty secret but I discovered nothing but the life work of a lady called Mariora Silver. Such thrilling titles they've got – *Bound in Captivity*, *The Gandolfi Letter* and *The Black Duke*. I opened one of them and read these words:

> She trembled in the shadow of the scented trees. Her eyelids closed and a great shivering sigh ran through her. She gasped for breath.
> "If only," he whispered.
> "No, no," she answered. "Everything must be just as it is."
> A deadly faintness crept over her. He caught her in his arms and the night of Mediterranean velvet enfolded them.
> "Soon," he whispered.
> "Now," she replied.

Well, really. What can I say? Gripping stuff. And who was Mariora Silver? And why was the tea chest abandoned in the attic?

*

Midnight.

All of a sudden I was reminded of the Nihilist women, the blonde renegades parading the decks of a Russian ironclad. What must it be like to travel so far, to go into imprisonment and exile as some women must?

Impelled to action, I rose quickly, sweeping out of the saloon. No-one noticed my departure except perhaps Madame Chrissavelonis, who is really very observant beneath her masque of charming languor.

On the deck I met Mr. Murat Bey, just as I expected.

He was striding up and down the port side of the steamer, carrying a copy of the *Strand Magazine*. I remembered the night when I had stood with him to watch the bright volcanic ash of Stromboli lighting the night air.

"I would like you to know, Madame, that I never seduced Miss Seawright."

This was amazingly direct. Even so, the news lightened my heart. I believed him at once.

"No?"

"No."

He hesitated for just an instant. He lit a cigar. The smell of his sulphurous match filled the air.

"Miss Seawright is playing an exceedingly dangerous game."

"Dangerous, Monsieur?"

"Very dangerous. Miss Seawright is a most accomplished manipulator."

I gazed out upon the dark sea. There was a hint of vapour in the air and from far away there came the forlorn wailing of a fog trumpet. Where was the island of Cythera, where Venus first stepped out of the foam? It did not occur to me to ask Mr. Murat Bey.

"Tell me, Monsieur. Whom is she manipulating?"

Mr. Murat Bey swept me with a look of astonishment. Lately, I have come to realize that this gentleman considers me to be a formidable woman. Neither beautiful nor susceptible, as I would like to be, but simply this – formidable. But if he supposes that I can follow his pattern of mind then he is quite wrong. He is, after all, foreign. It is only Englishmen whom I can be expected to understand.

"Her mother, Madame. Her mother, of course."

"Are mothers so very important? I haven't got one anymore, you see."

Smiling, Mr. Murat Bey fanned my face with his copy of the *Strand Magazine*. His voice is rather gravelly, not quite what I require, after all.

"Do not distress yourself, Madame. I expect that you get along very well without yours. And so will Miss Nettie, in my opinion."

In the time that it took me to return to my cabin I speculated on this. I undressed very quickly, scented bodice, white silk stockings and lace trimmed drawers sliding to the ground. Then I got out this notebook so that I could write everything down while it was still vivid and fragrant in my imagination.

The day after tomorrow we enter harbour at the port of Old Smyrna. Mrs. Seawright's famous dragoman will be waiting at the quayside. He is to accompany her to the Temple of Diana at Ephesus. I think that I am invited too.

While tomorrow night there is to be a moonlit dance.

*

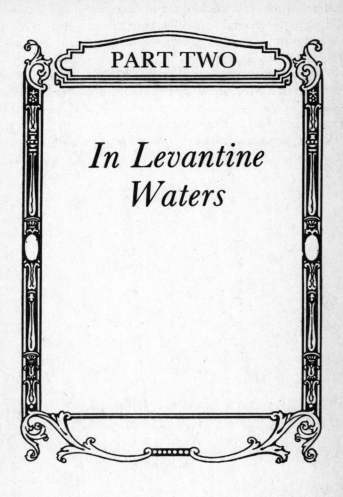

PART TWO

In Levantine Waters

How nasty and teasing diaries are. Mademoiselle Aimée was perfectly right: it is the dramatic moments of our lives which go unrecorded. I can find absolutely no trace of the moonlit dance.

There are no dance programmes to be found in the mahogany drawers and cobwebbed corners of the Cambridge house, no folded cards with tiny pencils attached by silken threads. The pages which describe the moonlit dance have been deliberately torn from the back of the petit journalier. I am looking down at the ragged edges right now. I picture illuminations; Adelina dancing a floating waltz with Mr. Murat Bey, perhaps inclining her soft cheek against his prickly one, a gesture which no-one remarks, while Rupert consoles himself with the beautiful, elegant Madame Chrissavelonis. Madame dances like an angel. She has a narrow waist, tightly bound, and her dancing slippers are silvery pale. They flash in the moonlight, dazzling Rupert. In the background the islands of the Sporades are replete with their own timeless stories, ominous in the velvety night. And as to the music, only the sad sweet songs of the nineties spring to my mind:

> After the Ball is Over
> After the Break of Day
> Many a Heart is Aching

Now that the house is empty of pictures, the carpets rolled up and the attic explored, there is a faint sweet smell of decay haunting the high-ceilinged rooms. It is the smell of an autumnal garden, rusty chrysanthemums, and papery unscented roses. The walls of the pantry are thick with verdigris mould. My estate agent has told me that the house has grown smelly, that visitors shudder as they march along the tiled hall. My great-great-grandfather's Gloire de Dijon rose rambles unpruned across the French doors of his study. The windows of the upstairs are crowded with wistaria.

I don't know why Granny allowed Professor Mackintosh's house to grow so cold and dilapidated but she was not a fastidious woman. She wore black silk underwear, occasionally rinsed in fragrant water. Granny was the sort of person who might well have stubbed out her cigarette in a pot of extravagant cold cream, as Mrs. Van Hopper does in *Rebecca*.

Granny died of a stomach tumour caused, I like to think, by smoking Gitanes. One Tuesday night she went to bed with a sharp stomach-ache and a tumbler full of Calvados and by the following Monday she was dead. I write 'I like to think' because otherwise I too might have this fate in store. I'm much too cowardly to smoke cigarettes. I am still informed by stories, especially bildungsroman, and I like to think that people who get stomach tumours deserve them.

Granny did not die in Cambridge but at Dieppe where Mr. Montieth, positively the last of her husbands, had left her an apartment in an elephant-coloured stone building along the seashore, not so very far from where the Dieppe Raid took place. Each of Granny's husbands was intended to be her last but it was only Mr. Montieth who managed this feat. Just the same, she was the only one who had a fondness for the house in Cambridge, having been brought up there by sharp-eyed Mrs. Bunn and the granite-eyed Professor.

I picture Mrs. Bunn always in black, with a face like a hatchet. I cannot imagine Mrs. Bunn all prepared for a moonlit dance, her neck dusted with powder, her hair brushed into elaborate loops, her eyelids painted and gleaming. In my own mind Mrs. Bunn is nothing but an apparition in the Professor's study, a figure holding a brass Indian tray and a pair of ratafia glasses all ready for the sticky nightcap which they shared every evening.

To my grandmother though dancing was a serious matter. She ran across each of her husbands at a dance. In 1942, at the age of forty-seven, Granny befriended an American master sergeant in order to perform the athletic new dances which were the special province of that gloomy year of English history. Her friendship with Sergeant Eiselbe was quite platonic; Granny always reserved her most enticing behaviour for well-to-do gentlemen. As with Mrs. Seawright, each of Granny's husbands left her richer than his predecessor had done. After the humiliating circumstances of her girlhood, what with arriving on the doorstep like a brown paper parcel one day, no-one quite knowing her exact lineage, Granny always took meticulous care to make sure that she was properly armoured against the vagaries of fortune. After her death in the apartment at Dieppe I discovered accounts at eight different financial institutions in England and France, every one of them for astonishing sums of money deposited on scandalously secure terms.

But now I've strayed from the subject of the dance which took place on board the steamer the night before the disembarkation at Smyrna. Perhaps it was on that very night that . . . But no. I have read on, after all, and the truth about Granny's birth is a bit of a shock. I have made one or two more discoveries though.

In the first place, I have found a certificate of marriage dated 1883. In the second place, I have got to the end of

Colonel Hevingham's file. On the very last page there is a copy of a yellowing newspaper cutting. It says this:

RENISHAW, Rupert
January 25th – Died of a coronary thrombosis on the floor of the Stock Exchange. Mr. Renishaw had been been in precarious health since his journey to Turkey in September last.

So she succeeded in giving Rupert a heart attack after all. Poor Rupert. How ruthless women are. But what newspaper was it in? And what year was it? I shall have to find out.

*

Friday, August 17th. Early morning. The Gulf of Smyrna. Little by little, I shall recount the entire day, Ephesus and all.

At dawn, I coaxed a glass of lemon tea from dark-visaged Angelina and took up my station on the deck. We churned by the volcanic island of Chios but Mr. Murat Bey, who is fond of volcanoes, did not appear.

Despite the early hour the air was velvety with warmth. The water was indigo and the sea birds visited me on the deck. I fed them crumbs of dry Parisian biscuits. There is no chance of sea-sickness now. The birds leapt and caroused on the oily deck, stealing crumbs from one another and shrieking victoriously.

Rupert snored below; he takes no delight in picturesque scenery. Even at the time of our honeymoon Rupert demanded that we visit the Low Countries, whereas I was determined on the splendours of the Norwegian fjords.

Soon Madame Chrissavelonis, wearing her rosy pearls, slipped out of her cabin. Monsieur is apparently at one with my husband in this matter. No island of Chios for either of them. Madame C. is descended, she told me, from the martyrs of Chios who were murdered by Vaid

Pasha at the time of the Greek War. Once the adventurous merchants of the island kept splendid palaces along the Campo but now they are burnt to ashes by the villainous Turks.

Madame Chrissavelonis was much affected by this story. She dabbed at her eyes with a scented mouchoir. Her eyes are glimmering pools of jet, they soften and flash by turns. She is very beautiful, very Sarah Bernhardt too. Her husband is not directly descended from the martyrs and this grave error sets her above him, I understand.

Wickedly, I enquired as to the whereabouts of Monsieur Georges.

"Below, Madame. Below. The late night, you see, and the raki too . . ."

Her words faded away, full of regret. She buried her handkerchief in the corners of her cherry-coloured velvet bag.

Neither of us were moved to exchange stories of our shipboard dance. She had waltzed a good deal with Rupert. I had fox-trotted quite a lot with Mr. Murat Bey though the Sultan does not, as a rule, permit his subjects to dance.

The thought of Monsieur Chrissavelonis groaning below, suffering the consequences of his own feast, made me consider more deeply the question of Madame's perfect happiness.

"Monsieur Chrissavelonis does not dance, does he?"

Madame shook her head.

"Nor play cards either?"

"Never," said Madame sadly.

A moment passed. Then Madame spoke once more.

"Gambling is for business, that is what Georges says. Not for pleasure."

Ah! Not perfectly happy after all. How this news warmed the cockles of my heart. Just the same, at least Georges had invested to advantage, whereas . . .

"They're monsters," I declared. "They never will share your pleasures. And it is what they are supposed to be for, after all."

"You must turn the tables on them," said Madame comfortingly. "It is what happens in Shakespeare."

This remark caught my attention immediately.

"Do you do that?"

"Yes, yes I do. In the kindest possible way, of course. I make a point of it. Life doesn't go on very long, you see."

Madame's gaze skimmed the surface of the sea. She raised a white hand to her dark eyes. Quite a lot of people would rather not consider the brevity of life. It gives them an awkward, prickly feeling. By this time Madame was smiling calmly, as if she knew rather a lot of things which I did not.

"And your other friend? Le Géant? He was not at the dance last night."

By le géant I understood that she meant Dickie, because he does rather resemble the leaning tower of Pisa, thin and poorly balanced as he is. I explained that moonlit dances were not in the least Dickie's favourite occupation, that he might have preferred something a touch milder – a tea party for disgracefully rich and raddled old ladies, for example, or on the other hand something altogether more CLEVELAND STREET.

Madame C. nodded sagely. It was only a polite enquiry. Although her own behaviour appears above suspicion, Madame is perfectly aware of how the rest of the world conducts itself.

I should, perhaps, record that the Gulf of Smyrna resembles nothing so much as a Scottish loch. We passed nearby an ancient Genoese battery which goes by the name of the Sanjak Katissi. I took out my sketchbook. Madame Chrissavelonis produced a weighty mahogany box, a black hood and tripod. While I employed my charcoals, she took the likeness of the Sanjak, a stern and devoted expression colouring her mild, sweet face.

62

"You are an accomplished photographer," I said.

"I am a passionate photographer," she replied.

It is strange how once you first begin to consider passion you find it everywhere, in Madame's photography, in Nettie's gooseberry eyes and Mr. Murat Bey's cigars. Love and affection are practically impossible to discover; they require nice judgement and dedication. Passion on the other hand is busy everywhere.

There was a pyramid of salt to be seen on the far beaches. Smyrna, at first, was nothing but a fine line of white traced on water of azure blue.

It requires a long while to take a likeness. Images impress themselves slowly; darkness is required. I did not speak again but only studied Madame's art. In the corner of my charcoal sketch I wrote: "For Dear Papa From His Loving Daughter Adelina."

Lately, it has occurred to me that I think too often of my father but this disquieting reflection did not cross my mind as I was sketching the Sanjak Katissi. It comes to me now as I am busy writing in my notebook. Indeed, I attempted to see the ancient battery with my father's eyes. I must ask Mrs. Seawright whether she was devoted to her own father, the intrepid circuit preacher.

"I shall keep a picture for you. To remind you of your journey to Smyrna."

"You must send it to the Summer Palace Hotel at Therapia. That is where Rupert and I are staying."

"I know. But we shall meet again in Stamboul," said Madame Chrissavelonis, her tender almond eyes rather beady just for once.

But how did she know? And what of her widowed mother-in-law and all the grand occasions prepared for her at Smyrna?

Such tactless questions as these caused Madame's eyes of jet to glitter. She shrugged her beautiful shoulders. She was full of indignation.

"I shall not devote my entire time to Georges's family. That would not do at all. Besides, my little girls must pay their visit to Saint Sophia's and the Museum of Antiquities. Flora would not remain with us otherwise. Flora is a decided believer in historical excursions."

And so am I, as a matter of fact.

*

The anonymous Victorian silhouette which was once my rendition of my great-grandmother Adelina's character has by now assumed detail and hue. I am beginning to detect a ruthless streak hidden deep within her. I can tell that as a character she outweighs Rupert, exceeds him, just as Granny exceeded all her rich husbands. Adelina's pale Shalimar hands are stained with violet ink. Her formidably high forehead was, I now know, inherited from Professor Mackintosh. Her mind was not empty as a bare cupboard, as I once imagined it to be, but was instead filled with a grand array of heroes and heroines.

I know that this sort of imagination is generally frowned on – my husband Sam was once heard to say that my entire picture of life was drawn from nineteenth century novels and 1930s movies. Just the same, I have always felt happiest when in the company of those who are on visiting terms with Elizabeth Bennet and Lily Dale, not to mention Tracy Lord or C. K. Dexter Haven. I am glad that Adelina and I have both known the many delights of the maroon chaise longue; it's a dying pleasure as everyone agrees.

But why didn't she marry her friend Mr. Walter Ramage, the gentleman who was so knowledgeable about particle theory and cricket? I do wish that she had. There is so much to be said for a soft-hearted husband.

Smyrna Cont.

There were sixty-seven people to meet Madame
Chrissavelonis at the harbour of Old Smyrna. I know
because I counted them. There were old ladies in their
sombre costumes, stout gentlemen puffing their aromatic
cigars, all of them joyful and astonishingly short. There
was even a band which played *God Save the Queen* and *La
Marseillaise* too, perhaps for our steamer and its crew.
Monsieur Georges was bleary-eyed from the drinking of
raki the night before. The little girls were solemn,
repeating their lines of Greek. Flora McPhee, their Scotch
nanny, exuded Calvinist composure. Like the elderly
Greek ladies she too wore garments of shiny black. It
occurred to me for the first time that my father would have
done better to choose a lady such as Flora McPhee to
bring me up. Then I would have been nourished with
useful facts and the tenets of good behaviour rather than
true stories of adventure and lying stories of swashbuck-
ling romance. I would not have spent so many afternoons
reading books and I would never have begun this diary.

"I shall accompany Mrs. Seawright to the Temple of
Diana," I told Rupert as we moored nearby the flooding
pontoons of the harbour.

Remember the scene at Marseilles, the squealing and
the ropes, the <u>smells</u>? It was all more pronounced at
Smyrna, I can tell you.

Rupert's hair was combed with a wet comb to either
side of his head. His collars and cuffs were especially white
and starchy. This morning he was his old self, mild-
mannered and judicious, not in the least peevish. I think
that the dance must have done him good.

"If you like, my dear. I shall be at the English Club with
Mr. Stavriti."

At every port, naturally, there is business for Rupert to
attend to and the thought of business always makes him

very cheerful. Mr. Stavriti is a renowned merchant of Smyrna, a famous benefactor of the city who was once a friend to old Mr. Renishaw. I do hope that he is of a shrewder character than Mr. Pullen at Marseilles and can offer Rupert sound advice.

Rupert began to speak of the family connection with Mr. Stavriti.

"He visited, you know, at Blackheath. He brought Greek brandy and poor old Father got completely . . ."

I think that Rupert might have been about to say 'blotto'. It was the sort of word which he might have chosen. Instead his attention was distracted by the sight of the watermen in their caiques and the white sails of the fishing vessels. It is true though, that people from quite outside the family were always coming and going at the Renishaw villa. I, too, was a visitor there, Kitty's best friend. That is how I first met Rupert and took it into my head to marry him.

People who claim that they cannot quite recollect just exactly why they married their particular husbands have always intrigued me. Some people do enjoy the thought that life is nothing but a series of random events. I am not like that at all. I am forever turning events to the light, looking for patterns and stories. There are only one or two reasons for getting married, after all. "I can't remember why I married him," they declare, their words brimming over with innocence and plaintiveness. It sounds rather like: "I can't remember just exactly *where* I found these old shoes of mine."

I married Rupert because he was Kitty's brother and because I wanted to run away from Papa and Mrs. Bunn and be decisive in my own household. Perhaps, too, I thought that our days would become like the ones in Blackheath, resounding to the notes of the pianola, thronging with animals and visitors and games of charades. In Blackheath people catch trains to the city, commit murders and exercise their dogs on the muddy grass. It is not at all like Cambridge where the men drink port together and go to their studies. I did not bargain for the maroon chaise longue and the books from Mudie's Circulating Library. Naturally I am very ashamed of myself, but there it is. I have written it down at last.

Luckily, Mr. Nicolopulo was waiting for us at the harbour. We went ashore in caiques, did I write that?

*

It was at a young ladies' academy in the Fenland town of March that my great-grandmother first met Rupert's sister, Kitty Renishaw. Kitty's girlhood passions subsided when she married Mr. Alston, a solicitor at Sheringham, and went to live in a three-storied flint house from which you can hear the crashing of the North Sea. As everyone knows, it is happiness which causes your ambitions to melt away like butter in the sunshine, not the opposite at all.

Adelina attended Bunyan Court because it was convenient and because Professor Mackintosh was by then anxious to have the house to himself. Kitty, I expect, was sent because it was cheap, the Renishaw finances having been in a desperate state long before poor Rupert became head of the firm. The school possessed a music mistress of some delicacy and talent, a certain Miss Rachel Cullimore. And Latin was taught with splendid vigour by Miss Harriet Layard. I know this because by an enormous stroke of luck I have discovered the letters which Adelina wrote to her father during the three years in which she was a pupil at Bunyan Court. I found them not in the mahogany wardrobe where the photographs were, but in a picnic hamper in what was once Adelina's dressing-room.

Kitty was a pianist of dash and inspiration while Adelina spent her evenings filling hard-backed Boots diaries with sensational stories of the sort which Professor Bhaer so discouraged Jo March from writing. When she returned to the confines of the Cambridge house, Adelina abandoned the Boots diaries. (I haven't found <u>them</u>. They remain to be discovered.) I like to think that there's a fictive vein to be met with in her volumes of travel memoirs, all those fierce bearded gentlemen, guides, interpreters and white-robed bearers who are the stuff of her pages. In her diary too, perhaps. But I'm always deathly suspicious of people's diaries. There is, after all, the celebrated case of Jane Welsh Carlyle, who only began a diary so as to revenge herself on her neglectful husband after she was dead – Thomas, if you remember, having been paying a good deal of attention to one Lady Ashburton at about that time.

But Mr. Nicolopulo, the celebrated dragoman, is about to make his entrance and once again I must imagine the scene. Adelina and the Seawright ladies are gingerly stepping out of their caique; Mr. Nicolopulo is dashing forward, a plump gentleman, perhaps as old as forty. His hair is smooth and shiny with brilliantine, not a single grizzled grey hair to be seen.

*

Friday the 17th. The Journey to Ephesus.

Descending on the quayside we took a cab as far as the Gare de la Pointe which stands at the northernmost tip of the port. It is the terminus of the Ottoman, Smyrna and Aidin Railway. But the cab progressed at the pace of a ceremonial elephant and even so we nearly ran down an ancient gentleman who was endeavouring to sell a packet of antique bronze coins to Mrs. Seawright.

"I beg you, Madame," said Mr. Nicolopulo. "You must be firmness itself."

But she was not. In any case, Mr. Nicolopulo's tone was far too gentle for discouragement. The sight of such poor people afflicted Mrs. Seawright. In the end she bought the packet of coins.

"Madame, Madame," scolded Mr. Nicolopulo, full of sorrow.

Mrs. Seawright was not in the least downcast.

"I think that we might view the city," she declared. "Before catching our train."

How very odd that she is nothing but putty in the hands of beggars and penniless tutors but quite imperious when it comes to the rest of us. On occasion, Mrs. Seawright sounds like a great Shakespearian actress. Her voice positively throbs with command.

I could tell that Mr. Nicolopulo was going to turn out a malleable man because he was perfectly agreeable to this, never mentioning the fact that we were likely to miss our train, the Temple of Diana express.

Instead he was touched and delighted that a rich foreign lady was taking such a deep interest in his native city. He brandished his straw hat in the air as if he had conjured up this spectacle for our pleasure alone.

"You see before you, Madame, the great Byzantine port of Smyrna. An antique city, Madame. A city of the Bible. A city of genius."

You can see why he is a famous dragoman. Inside Mr. Nicolopulo there is always excitement bubbling, pride and pleasure too.

"You will understand it all, ladies, when we are finished together. All will be revealed. The East is mine!"

Naturally, he is the sort of man who is inclined to be carried away. The East is very far from being his; he is nothing but a shabby dragoman and teacher of Greek. Just the same, his words are so very delightful and theatrical.

Did I mention that I admired Mr. Nicolopulo from the

very beginning? It is the truth. I took to him immediately. I adored him. I liked his hands especially. They're very elegant and bony. Later on I shall describe his voice.

*

In those days Smyrna was still a Greek city, bathed in a clear Hellenic light. There was a Greek hospital where lunatics calmly paraded the stone-flagged passages. There was a Greek school too. At this school raven-haired spinsters of a high-minded disposition pronounced their lessons. In one of the classrooms there hung a portrait of Mr. Gladstone, white-whiskered and full of righteousness. The English, at that time, were kindly regarded by the Greeks because William Gladstone had had the fore-thought to return the Ionian islands to the Hellenic government rather than stealing them for Queen Victoria as Disraeli might have done. Hospitals and schools being the foundations of civilization they were, at that time, associated irredeemably with the English.

Smyrna thronged with the steamships of the world as well as ingenious doctors. There were wooden houses, delicate and beautiful as painted eggs, apt to catch fire. There were the mineral waters too, the Baths of Agamem-non, and a collection of clubs – the Oriental Club where there was caviar and a Russian dish of salmon and rice to be had and the English Club, famous for its Singapore curry and Yorkshire puddings, the sort of place where Rupert, conducting his meeting with Mr. Stavriti, must have felt very much chez lui . . .

Nowadays though, like so many cities which lie in an easterly direction, Smyrna has acquired another name and is known, after the Turkish fashion, as Ismir.

Once upon a time, Sam and I arrived in Ismir and we too visited the Baths of Agamemnon. On account of the subterranean heat the land is noted for its fertility. The

70

hot springs form in a cleft of the mountains nearby the city and there is no reason at all to connect them with Agamemnon. But Sam, who studied classical matters at school and is intrigued by water in all its forms, insisted upon the expedition. In those days, I overflowed with love for him and so, as you might expect, I agreed.

*

Journey to Temple of Diana. Friday 17th cont.

On the train to Ephesus Mr. Nicolopulo came to sit beside me. He is a personal dragoman of the highest order, a Thomas Cook dragoman, but men like Mr. Nicolopulo never do grow rich or well-connected. He is writing his own guide to the city of Constantinople which will appear very soon. Mrs. Seawright has booked a cabin for him; he is to travel with us to Constantinople and then return to Smyrna after the expedition to the Trojan plains.

I could not help noticing that Nettie was rather wan, a little reduced in spirits, after a flagrant indulgence in the dottore's medicine cabinet. Sometimes I think that it might be better to allow Nettie to marry the young man who is heir to a railroad fortune for, as Mrs. Phineas Finn did her best to explain to the Duke of Omnium, girls generally do end by getting their own way in matters of this sort.

As for Mrs. Seawright herself, (Mr. Nicolopulo addresses her with deliberate courtesy, always calling her 'chère Madame') the climate does not agree with her. She too, was in a fragile condition, her eyes glazed and her cheeks a distressing shade of scarlet. Neither of them was in a fit state to delight in the Temple of Diana, as I certainly was.

Soon Mr. Nicolopulo began to speak of his family. All Greeks do speak of their families, Madame Chrissavelonis had warned me. Just the same, I was perfectly at ease with Mr. Nicolopulo. I was glad too that he had come to sit beside me. As he spoke of his children, he pointed out the ruins of ancient settlements to me, flashing his brown hands against the window pane. I like it when knowledge is given to me, the very best of presents.

"I have four daughters, Madame. Such exquisite children. They sing like birds. They are goodness itself."

I pictured Mr. Nicolopulo's daughters, their sweet voices and their thick curly dark hair. I even went so far as to invent names for them: Mariora, after Madame Chrissavelonis, and perhaps a grave little Henrietta, a plump Despina and a gurgling baby Julia.

Mr. Nicolopulo has a passion for the novels of Sir Walter Scott. He was carrying a small volume of burgundy-coloured leather in one of his deep and rumpled pockets.

"I am reading *Ivanhoe* to my daughters."

He spoke proudly.

"They do understand, you know."

Lucky Mr. Nicolopulo. What miraculous, clever girls. My dear friend, Kitty – who lives in the bracing climate of Sheringham, nearby the North Sea – has two little boys. Their names are Rupert and Arthur. I did not know that Kitty was fond enough of her brother to name a child after him. She was astonished when I said that I was going to marry Rupert. She even went so far as to advise me against it. Strongly too.

"Marry Rupert!" she said. "What a silly idea! How very brainless of you! Really! And how did you come by it? Is it something that you've been reading, Addie? *Little Women*, perhaps? Or was it Mrs. Humphrey Ward?"

Kitty was always very scathing about my reading matter. When she was a girl she could be very rude. She is far more circumspect now that she is married to a lawyer.

"Of course you don't know what you're doing," she

snapped when I told her that I had already made up my mind. "You're far too innocent."

In those days Kitty had wonderfully long hair which crinkled down to her knees and eyes as bright as jewels. But Kitty herself has grown rather bracing nowadays and Mr. Alston, her husband, is so gentle and companionable that she has no time for other people at all.

"I have no children at all. Not a single one."

Mr. Nicolopulo treated this confidence with the sympathy and gravity which I thought it deserved. He nodded solemnly and said nothing at all. I expect that he knew about my childless state. You can always tell. People without children have so much less to talk about, quite the opposite of what you think when you are young.

As our train chuntered in a southerly direction, specks of coal dust descending on Nettie's sweet white dress, Mr. Nicolopulo began speaking again. His voice was rather deep, his words fell slowly, one by one, not unlike French dictation. They rippled down my spine. They caused my hands to tremble. Can simple words do this?

By now Mrs. Seawright was snoring deeply, her head lolling against the antimacassar. Nettie, who has borrowed my Ouida, was deeply enthralled. From time to time shadows of delight and passion danced across her milky face. Now and again she shivered. I felt quite alone with Mr. Nicolopulo, quite alone and perfectly happy.

"Beyond Ephesus there is fig growing country and the celebrated ruins of Heirapolis. Laodicea. I expect you have heard of the Laodiceans?"

I have heard of Laodice, the wife of Antiochus II, for whom the city was named. When her husband cast her off, as sometimes husbands do, she raised a mighty army in order to murder the son of her Egyptian rival, Berenice. She was not at all the sort of woman to bear an insult.

By now people were jumping up from their seats, slamming shut their books and retrieving their Gladstone bags. Nettie was lapped in a sea of romantic melodrama, the pupils of her eyes were dark as those of a cat dreaming in the shadows. Beside her, Mrs. Seawright was wriggling her toes and groaning.

Mr. Nicolopulo leant in my direction. He smelled agreeable and spicy. He made me smile.

"There, Madame. We have reached Ayasouluk. Do you see the castle on the hill?"

Yes, a Byzantine castle on a brown hilltop. I saw it quite plainly.

"And don't forget your bag, Madame. Here it is."

With great solemnity, Mr. Nicolopulo handed me my muslin bag. It is full of notebooks and charcoals.

"No, oh no. Thank you."

"And now, dear ladies, we must see about our donkeys."

Mr. Nicolopulo <u>does</u> affect me in a very odd way. He is exactly the opposite of the scornful Mr. Murat Bey who has, by the way, left the *Tigre* without saying goodbye to me.

*

'Affect' indeed. I've noticed too that Adelina's prose is 'affecting' my own so that I'm beginning to write 'disquiet' when what I really mean is bloody furious. And I shouldn't become too carried away by the spectacle of the redoubtable ladies of the past, wriggling across glaciers in their hobble skirts, galloping through the high table lands of Central Asia in their bustles and stays. They got away with murder. I myself happen to know of at least one who travelled 'alone' through Africa while accompanied by entire armies of wretched, sickly native servants. In those days English scorn wrapped the entire world. My London Library reading has revealed that yet another renowned female traveller journeyed all the way

74

to Anatolia simply in order to observe that there was not one single plant there which did not grow better in England. After all, there is a school of thought which would maintain that stringing out your life in a series of unnecessary journeys is a very advanced form of passivity indeed.

I know why I married Sam. Adelina isn't the only one capable of truth. We're not all liars nowadays. I married Sam because I loved him and because I required him to declare that he intended to devote the rest of his life to me. It is monstrous but there it is, the unvarnished truth. I didn't believe in marriage. I still don't. It was something I <u>wanted</u>, not something I <u>believed in</u>.

Sam was not entirely agreeable to the notion of marrying me. In the end though I did have my way with him. I've got a ruthless streak too. The ceremony followed the visit to the Aegean. What I can't remember just at present is why I divorced him. I did love him, you see. The emotions of the past, unlike letters and dance programmes, are quite impossible to resurrect. But in any case, I think that it was my friend Julia's advice which was decisive. In those days Julia was an unmarried woman herself, what is more she was a psychological social worker and as a consequence took quite a tepid view of matrimony.

The thing is, nowadays your friends cannot be expected to sympathize with a catalogue of complaints about your husband. This used to be what friends were for. Not anymore though. They simply say: "Get rid of him." It isn't as if Sam had injured me in any way. He hadn't. Sam is kind and clever. We used to drink wine together in the evenings and talk about Trollope novels.

But there are those who favour continuity in life, and those who take great delight in change. And at that time, I am afraid to say, I was the one who was tempted by change.

Continued.

At Ayasouluk station, Mr. Nicolopulo hired three donkeys for us in order that we should make our way to the Temple of Diana. Mine was a gentle mooning creature with brown eyes. Nettie's, on the other hand, was very fierce, while Mrs. Seawright's donkey was especially broad-backed and plodding.

Mr. Nicolopulo told us that the temple counted among the seven wonders of the ancient world and that its building was commenced five hundred and forty one years before the time of Christ. It was constructed in the midst of a noxious marsh on foundations, they say, of charcoal and the fleece of sheep. Later on the temple was plundered by horridly disreputable Nero and afterwards, set to the torch by the Goths.

Dear Mr. Nicolopulo recounted these enthralling events in a tone of mellow horror. As in the train his words fell one by one, delightfully. Faint beads of sweat appeared on his brow. It is plain that the ancient world horrifies Mr. Nicolopulo.

"Here, chère Madame, the black arts flourished. In May, all Asia came to celebrate their pagan festivals."

Shards of antique pottery caught the light. Blocks of recalcitrant stone lay in crumpled attitudes. When Mr. Woods came here to investigate the terrain in 1874 there was nothing to be seen but hillocky, tussocky land. He was our Consul at Smyrna, a man evidently less absorbed in the exercise of his profession than is my husband.

"The people of Ephesus were celebrated for their worship of the dead."

"Necromancy," said Mrs. Seawright sharply.

All this time Nettie was seated beneath her white parasol attending dreamily to my Ouida novel. I think that she liked it. From time to time she would give a faint little gasp, her cheeks turning rosy. Very occasionally she

76

would dart a glance in my direction, twitching her fine, light eyebrows as she did so.

"Are you enjoing it, Nettie?"

"I think I am. It's hard to be sure. I'm not certain that it's meant to be <u>enjoyed</u> in quite that way though."

Of course philosophers have debated for centuries as to whether our passions can be said to be enjoyed or not. I mentioned this to Nettie.

"Oh, philosophers . . ."

Nettie wrinkled her nose which, despite the shelter of a shady brown bush and elaborate white hat, was on the point of turning pink.

"Mr. Nicolopulo says that it was Amazons who founded the Temple of Diana."

I had made the mistake of supposing that Amazons might appeal to Nettie, young and lithe and female as she was.

"You see, Mrs. Renishaw, I'm not really interested in Amazons. And I don't like anything which is old or broken."

It is plain that Nettie is neither shocked by the ancient world nor intrigued by it. It does not touch her in the slightest. These stones, this light, do not affect her any more deeply than the backdrop at the Piccadilly Theatre.

"And you don't like journeys either, do you?"

"No. Not a scrap."

In the novels which I read, American girls do not say, "Not a scrap". Mrs. Seawright has turned Nettie into a girl without a country. Henry James would not recognize her. You cannot help wondering what the Chicago meat packer would have made of her.

In a voice which was clear and sweet, Nettie proclaimed: "I would rather like to become a society hostess."

Children never do seem to want anything but the very things from which their loving parents have delivered them. I wondered whether Mr. Nicolopulo had realized this yet, how soon it will be before his little daughters begin to express their scorn for Sir Walter Scott.

Not far away, as it happens, Mr. Nicolopulo was instructing Mrs. Seawright. His voice on this occasion was rather baritone, his black straw hat crumpled under his arm.

"Ephesian letters, Madame, carved into the bases of wicked statues . . . No doubt Madame remembers the story of Demetrius the silversmith."

I knew at once that Mrs. Seawright <u>did</u> remember the story. She was a little dusty, a touch fatigued. Still, she remembered the story of the silversmith. I expect that she first heard it from her father, perhaps at a camp meeting in Kansas on a starry evening full of fireflies.

She began to recite in such a dramatic fashion that even Nettie looked up, blinking underneath her shady hat.

"'Moreover ye see and hear that not alone at Ephesus but throughout all Asia this Paul hath persuaded and turned away people, saying that they be no gods which are made with hands . . .'"

Mr. Nicolopulo was enchanted. His dark eyes glowed. The moment before he had been a plump and soulful little man with brilliantined hair. Now he was a dashing orator, lit by the fire of biblical poetry, rushing in to cap Mrs. Seawright's quotation.

I expect that that is why St. Paul came to Ephesus, the Ephesians <u>were</u> so monstrously wicked. And their cult was a feminine one, that has to be admitted. St. Paul, as everybody knows, was famously scornful of females. Naturally, Mr. Nicolopulo is a Christian, much keener on St. Paul than on the goddess Diana.

On the way back in the dusty train he whistled Verdi arias, Walter Scott and Verdi being his favourites. He is evidently a great romantic, Mr. Nicolopulo. I, on the other hand, wrote these very pages in my Parisian notebook. You can even see the traces of sweat from the pads of my fingers, the gentle smearing of my navy blue ink.

*

Like Adelina's Mr. Ramage, Sam is a physicist. He is also American, like Mrs. Seawright, though why he remains in England is a mystery to me. For one thing, physicists are not esteemed in this country. No science please, we're British. For another, he's not a man without a country. He can only bear so many insults. The notion that the English are polite is, Sam says, a quite untruthful one. If good manners are what you require then America is definitely the place to go. But I suspect that Sam, like Mr. Murat Bey, is rather absorbed by the spectacle of a society in the final throes of utter decay. English roads and English showers are his special subjects.

Sam knows all about Adelina though. I've sent him a xerox copy of her first volume, the journey as far as the Gulf of Smyrna. He'll be delighted to find that Adelina has finally outgrown Mr. Rochester figures – brooding, bearded gentlemen with mad wives; sweetbriar and southernwood, do I smell the scent of Mr. Rochester's cigar? He has even invited me to stay at his cottage in Wells for the weekend. I'm not in the least sure that I'll go though.

I am visiting my friend Julia next week. She is marketing director for a communications company nowadays and she specializes in the selling of books with shimmering gold covers. Sex and shopping books, they are called.

"Just like Ouida," Julia told me once. But it isn't true at all. Ouida was altogether more diverting and not in the least interested in shopping.

It's the grounding in psychology which makes Julia such a gifted salesman, she told me that herself. She's had rather a brilliant career since she abandoned social work. Whereas she used to be very poor she is now very rich. She has a house with plum trees in the garden and a conservatory with red and black tiles. It was five storeys tall, the last time I counted. Out of her drawing-room window there is a Sickert painting of misty North London to be seen, not at all like my flat from which you can see the arching gateway of a Victorian funeral parlour. In Normandy, Julia has another house where the chairs are painted yellow and the wistaria flowers like bunches of dark grapes. There's an orchard of cider apples and a meadow too.

I ought to be able to turn this Adelina stuff into <u>something</u>, oughtn't I?

*

Mrs. Seawright's accident.

Upon our return to the Gare de la Pointe there was an enormous, smelly crush. A party of Turkish soldiers was gathered on the platform. The air was steamy, thick with coal smoke. The soldiers were lean with brown faces, very handsome. Little children with dusty feet squatted on the ground and veiled ladies turned their faces to the wall in order to eat sweetmeats of honey and almond paste. There was even a dwarf selling black aromatic coffee from a brass trolley. I loved it all; Mr. Nicolopulo did not.

"Wait till you see Stamboul," he said gloomily. "This is nothing."

In the Orient ladies wear pads of thick cotton under their arms in order to absorb their sweat. The difficulty is that these pads are horribly uncomfortable and give you a rash as well. I was speculating about this when Mrs. Seawright slipped on the platform and fell to her knees. There was a dreadful crashing sound. Suddenly her face turned white; she was grinding her teeth together.

"No bones snapped, I think," said Mr. Nicolopulo.

"No-o," whimpered Mrs. Seawright.

"Do let me have a look," said Nettie bossily.

It is so very humiliating to fall down. I think that at first Mrs. Seawright was more put out by the indignity than by the agony.

Staunchly, Mr. Nicolopulo gripped her elbow though he is a fragile man and this was rather a cumbersome operation for him.

"Chère Madame."

"I'm quite all right, thank you. Please don't fuss. A little fresh air is all I need."

Nettie was delving in her muslin bag, throwing down rouge and handkerchieves, my Ouida and a silver-backed hair brush. A portrait photograph too, I happened to notice. Not of Mr. Murat Bey, but of someone else entirely. A young man with silky hair and stern light eyes.

You would not think that Nettie had been dreaming in the train just a moment before. She was springy as a dislodged cat. Soon she found what she was searching for.

"A fan. Just the thing, Mama."

Next she waved a bottle of reviving salts under her mother's nose, the picture of efficiency. Bitter scent wafted through the air. Mrs. Seawright shuddered.

"Now, dear Madame. You must lean on me once again."

Mr. Nicolopulo was rosy with exertion. Mrs. Seawright was busy being brave.

Without a breath of thought Nettie knelt down, swept back the white ruffles of her flannel travelling skirt and unhitched a silvery silk stocking. Triumphant, she brandished the stocking in the air where it attracted quite a lot of keen glances.

Mr. Nicolopulo averted his gaze. He was smiling though, I could tell. I expect he has seen a good many silk stockings in his time. The soldiers on the other hand began to stamp their boots and whistle through their fingers.

Nettie was quite undisturbed.

"We'll bind up your ankle, Mama. Turkish soldiers are fearful brutes, Madame Chrissavelonis warned me."

Kneeling on the dirty hot ground in her white clothes, Nettie wound the stocking around her mother's ankle.

Mrs. Seawright was touched and surprised.

"Dear child. How capable you are. I never knew."

Mr. Nicolopulo murmured, "Brava, brava."

"I learned at Miss Favour's, you see. And it's very straightforward."

In a cab smelling quite strongly of beer we returned to the harbour, Mrs. Seawright groaning and Mr. Nicolopulo whistling a song from *Iolanthe*. *Iolanthe*, as Mr. Nicolopulo pointed out, is not Verdi but it does have its place.

At 7.30 the screw of our steamer began to twirl in preparation for our departure from the harbour of Old Smyrna. Nettie came down to dinner on her own. She was wearing a brilliant emerald ring on her finger. It matched her eyes wonderfully and glinted in all directions. Mrs. Seawright had not told me that the heir to the railroad fortune (for who else could it have been?) had given Nettie a priceless ring.

*

As I have mentioned before, my friend Julia is a woman who begins her life freshly every three or four years. Successfully too. Once, as I have said, she was a psychological social worker who advised me to divorce my husband Sam. We went for a walk in Hyde Park together. It was spring, the grass was thick with starry crocuses; at least, that's how I remember it. I expect that Dickie Ricardo would have felt that the condition of the flowers in Hyde Park was quite incidental. The wind carried the faint sweet scent of early blossoms.

Julia said: "He's getting to be a bit of a bore. I'd divest if I were you."

Julia is tall and skinny. She is capable of great disdain, especially for people who are not as skinny as she is. Julia maintains that while everybody cannot be rich and successful they can at least do their utmost to be <u>thin</u>.

"He's writing a book. Books do take a long time to write, you know."

Julia sighed. "Yes, but he's been working on it for three years now, hasn't he? And don't you think that there are enough books? Books are a terrible bore, after all."

It's a proposition certainly. I proposed it to myself. Lovely books can be a bore. Old dusty books with cracked bindings; crisp jolly paperbacks and cloth-bound clean copies: all nothing but a bore. I thought of austere and narrow Penguins in criminal green and travelling cherry pink. There was a time when people like Julia considered books to be elitist, a far more diabolical crime than that of simply being boring.

"I'm still considering. Not good ones. They aren't a bore."

"Anyway, I've given you the benefit of my advice."

Advice is not hard to come by, just expensive. I've been doing without it since 1985.

I went to see Julia in her office yesterday. The weather is milder than the day on which I went to see Colonel Hevingham. I couldn't help remembering that in the country there would be misty patches of bluebells under the trees, horse chestnuts coming into flower too. In London, on the other hand, it was not unlike the station at Smyrna, thronging with people, gritty and smelly. There are beggars too nowadays, something you would never have seen in my nineteen-fifties childhood when Granny used to put on her gloves and take me by train to see the White Tower and Madame Tussaud's.

Julia has thick dark hair, cut rather sternly, just like

Katherine Mansfield's. She was wearing a long cashmere cardigan with floppy pockets, thick red lipstick too. This is not the kind of thing she used to wear when she was young but I don't comment about people's clothes nowadays. There was a 1930s radio in her office, the sort which lights up warmly and has rounded corners.

I asked her advice about Adelina.

"I'd write a biography if I were you. Intrepid explorer. Lots of pictures. Did she or didn't she. <u>You</u> know."

"I think she might have done," I conceded. "But only just occasionally."

"There you are then. That's the stuff."

I was surprised at Julia. When we first met she was fourteen years old and used to read *Chalet School* stories in the bath at nights. If she fancied something a little more risqué then it was Georgette Heyer. "Do we have to talk about *that* all the time?" she used to say.

"Why is it that we're so delighted by the passions of our forebears, Julia?"

"Because that's how <u>we</u> came about, of course."

Julia was very brisk. I could tell that she was busy. I was on the point of asking if she had ever heard of a novelist called Mariora Silver but I decided against it.

"Naturally I've always envied people who could write about their relations for a living . . . Just the same . . ."

"Writers write you know, Penelope. They don't sit around leafing through picnic hampers and making up excuses for not getting on with the job. This vogue for female explorers isn't going to last. Windows in the market don't stay open forever, you know."

"Just the same, I'm not entirely sure that it's honest."

"Honest! Honestly. You sound just like Sam. Money's what counts nowadays."

I was doing my best to concentrate on Julia's wonderful radio and not think about money counting. Anyway at Crick, Frick they say that it's information which counts.

Marcus tells Victoria so every day. I think that he's been telling her at night as well but that is only a suspicion. I love old radios. There's nothing quite like them. When I was a student I had an enormous one. It stood in the middle of my narrow room. I even used to polish it with beeswax from time to time. You could eat from it, write on it too. I expect that Julia has forgotten my radio. People who are always having new lives generally do forget the old ones. I should mention perhaps that Julia is a married woman now; she has lots of children and a nanny called Tatiana. I don't think that she altogether approves of the fact that I'm divorced, she has asked me not to discuss the details with her children.

Obviously she remembers Sam though.

"I'd thought of writing a novel instead."

It struck me, you see, that this was the honest way out. If you can't write the exact truth about the past, if you have a weakness for embroidery despite all your education, then why not confess that it's all pretend anyway?

Julia looked amazingly stern.

"Darling Penelope. It takes <u>talent</u> to write fiction."

When you work for Crick, Frick the clients don't address you like this. They tremble when you cross the threshold. I began to think about windows in the market. I began to think of abandoning Adelina's notebooks and returning to a proper job. I've been calling in to say that I'm ill rather a lot lately. Marcus raises his eyebrows when I step out of the elevator in the mornings. When I was married to Sam, he used to phone in for me as he has a very deep and convincing tone of voice. Living by yourself though you feel the need to cough and quaver, otherwise the secretaries won't believe you. Victoria is very stern with people who malinger.

Julia kissed my cheek when I left.

"Goodbye darling. Do work hard, won't you? Rome wasn't built in a day, you know."

She seemed a little flustered. Her phone was already ringing. Everyone seems to think that my life is in a muddle. My mother used to think so, I could glimpse it in her eyes. I don't know why they worry about me. Money is what counts, they all say, and I've got enough of that.

I'm seeing Sam myself as it happens. Next weekend. I think I'll go by train from Liverpool Street, the way I always used to.

*

Saturday August 18th, 1894. Hellespont and Sea of Marmora.

I was awake at dawn to see the island of Mitylene which is renowned for its beauty. Nevertheless I am not going to describe it just yet. I've got something else to recount and I'm doubtful as to how to go about it. It is rather a delicate topic and I am boiling with rage. Perhaps I ought to dive in, not paddle around on the edges of disclosure. That's what Rupert did when he told me about it, after all. He simply plunged in without a breath of ceremony.

I'm drinking a tumbler of Doctor Banti's tonic just now as a matter of fact. Otherwise I'd be suffering from palpitations. Until you reach a certain age palpitations are nothing but imagination. Then they become quite real, your hearts thunders in your chest, in your ears too. I need quite a lot of Doctor Banti's elixir if I'm to survive. It's principally alcohol by the flavour of it but it's in a discreet brown bottle. Doctor Banti makes up excellent powders too. First rate for headaches. Mrs. Seawright is taking the tonic for her injured ankle. Lydia Pinkham's, she calls it.

*

I know what happens next. It's to do with that marriage certificate that I discovered in the bottom of the picnic hamper, the secret marriage which I mentioned at the beginning of this notebook. Jane Eloise Bunn and James Louis Mackintosh. 1883. Adelina is about to discover the truth about her beloved Papa. But of course it's all blindingly obvious. I can't imagine why she didn't work it out for herself. Think of how Mademoiselle Aimée was sent away to Lyons and Adelina bundled into the charge of Miss Harriet Layard, the brisk Latin scholar. And consider one or two of the previous entries in the notebooks, how the very mention of Professor Mackintosh is guaranteed to turn Rupert livid with rage.

I always knew that there was something fishy going on in that tall cold house. I ought to find out what those foggy yellow bricks were made out of. Then I would understand why they attract so much water. I expect Dickie Ricardo knew about the marriage all along. I expect he had tried to tell Adelina on several occasions. Dickie would have made a legendary spy, blackmailer too, I expect.

*

Revelazione.

As I was sitting up in bed very late last night pasting postcards into my album (I've acquired fine hand-tinted views of the Temple of Diana and the seething harbour of Old Smyrna) I happened to mention how very much Papa would have enjoyed Ephesus and how he would have got on with Mr. Nicolopulo too. Like the best of rationalists Papa is a dab hand at the Bible. I expect he knows all about St. Paul and Demetrius the silversmith.

As I say, I mentioned this to Rupert even though he was rather doing his best to fall asleep. It is the effect which my voice generally has on him. He finds it very soporific.

"Papa, Papa," Rupert groaned, accidentally knocking off his tasselled nightcap as he did so. "Do we have talk about Papa just now? Why not . . ."

It does not matter what the subject under discussion, now is never the proper time. I carried on staunchly. I mentioned Laodice and the infamous Antiochus II.

In the meanwhile Rupert's hands had begun to glide over me. There was a certain dreamy expression on his face which I recognized. "What lovely breasts you've got, Adelina. What silky hair."

From an old husband (or perhaps I should say *ancien*, as the French do, in order to indicate long-standing rather than decrepitude) this sort of thing is rather surprising. Of course Madame Chrissavelonis has splendid creamy upright breasts. I expect that Rupert has noticed them. Mine are better though, no doubt about it.

"The thing about Papa . . ."

At this second interruption Rupert's face blazed with colour and he began to tell me the truth about my celebrated Papa. I think that he must have been saving up the news for ages and ages. Once he began he got going strongly right away. There was a vein beating menacingly in his neck. I think that he enjoyed himself, revealing Papa's secret. It did not take him very long.

Rupert told me that Papa and Mrs. Bunn have been married for more than ten years now and that Mrs. Bunn has her own house in Alpha Road. There's a child too, Rupert says. According to Rupert the marriage was kept a secret because Papa did not want the other Fellows to know that he had married a provision merchant's widow who had once been a lady's maid.

"But it can't be true. You're only saying it because you're so cross."

"No, oh no. Gospel."

"Why didn't they tell me?" I cried, working myself up as best I could.

"Come along now, Addie. Don't aggravate my dyspepsia. Take it like a man."

"You should drink Eno's."

Generously, I overlooked the part about being a man. I did not want to aggravate his dyspepsia any further.

"Should I?"

"Of course you should. And they should have told me."

Rupert was smiling. It was a smug smile, a little turned-up smile. I had kept him awake, pasting in my views of Ephesus and Smyrna and, as I have said before, he has never admired Papa. He was eager to secure revenge.

"I don't suppose that they thought you wanted to know."

Rupert said this in a nasty, self-important sort of voice, as though I did not have proper feelings as other people do.

I turned the matter over in my mind. I even thought of allowing one or two crystal tears to glide down my cheeks but this would only have disturbed Rupert horribly. It's not that Rupert would laugh, as Mr. Murat Bey would. Rupert would not do that. It is just that he believes that women only shed tears in order to drum up sympathy. He has never noticed that it is a sign of anger.

"Come along now, my dear. Do make an effort." Rupert was rather urgent, past the dreamy stage by now.

If only he would not wear a tasselled nightcap. If only he would not call me 'my dear'. If only . . .

"Do we have to do this just now? Is it absolutely necessary?"

Rupert blinked, stopped what he was doing.

"Oh, I think so, don't you? There's a good girl."

It's the deception which astonishes me. Papa is supposed to be a rationalist, a man of science. He observes the phenomena. Why would he do this? People can be so very mysterious, even clever ones.

"If you would, Rupert, if you could, do take off your nightcap, please."

"Adelina. My nightcap."

"And your nightshirt."

"There. Oh!"

I forgot to say that when all this was over (not quickly at all, it all took far longer this time) I had a wonderful idea for a piece of romantic fiction. I got out my violet ink right away and began writing the first scene. It's all going to be very Gothic. It's the story of a beautiful young heiress obliged to run away from her wicked and avaricious step-father, a man who only wants to sell her in marriage. I think that there ought to be a Balkan count in the story, a Turkish pirate too. I expect that the Turkish pirate will grow more and more like Mr. Murat Bey with every word I write. I expect that he will smoke cigars and have a sardonical air. The heiress of course resembles no-one so much as Miss Nettie Seawright. She is tall and pale and fond of Liberty prints. She has Nettie's green eyes and lofty gaze.

But how shall I end my story? I do not know yet. Nothing is easier than making people up. Endings are the impossible part as everyone agrees.

*

In the cold spring rain yesterday I visited the National Portrait Gallery. I got very wet, my cheeks were fiery – as though I had been drinking champagne – and my shoes slid on the grey pavement in Trafalgar Square. There's nowhere like the Portrait Gallery though, no rain like English rain.

I went to study the faces of the men of science, to peer at them and absorb their mysteries. I thought that perhaps they would lend me some insight into the character of James Louis Mackintosh. I've never examined them before. I used to walk right past them with my nose in the air. I'd never heard of Lord Kelvin until I met Sam. I always relied on Sam for useful scientific information. One snowy afternoon as we lay in bed, languorously entwined, he explained the second law of thermodynamics to me. The first is straightforward, it says that energy is neither created nor destroyed, that it's always there and always the same. The second law is rather more slippery.

"But you see, the capacity of energy to do *work* is forever diminishing," Sam explained, elaborating a series of delightful pictures – water running through mill streams and descending rocky falls. "The universe itself is running down, getting doddery and . . ."

"So that what we're doing now . . ."

"Oh yes. That uses up tremendous quantities of capacity."

"And that's why boxers . . ."

You see, I got the hang of it in the end. I've forgotten lots of things which Sam taught me, but not the life of Lord Kelvin or the second law of thermodynamics.

That afternoon Sam made Lapsang tea for me in a rosy Chinese teapot. Sam could always do things like make tea or skin a sole. He is a man of practicality as well as intellect. It made me feel de trop sometimes, as though he were quite sufficient by himself. Sam cut chunks of gingerbread to go with the tea. All the time the snow was falling straight down in thick, creamy goosefeathers, I haven't forgotten that either.

In any case, there I was at the Portrait Gallery inspecting Lord Kelvin and remembering Sam.

Did I mention that Granny used to take me to Madame Tussaud's? When I was older she took me to the Portrait Gallery. It's a sad thing but you do grow out of Madame Tussaud's. One day the waxen people begin to appear dead and recalcitrant while the painted ones at the portrait gallery begin to seem alive and alight. Both institutions are dedicated to the proposition that character prevails over circumstances. It isn't inexorable forces that you've got to worry about, it's inexorable people.

Of all the great men of British science only Sir

Humphrey Davy was renowned for his handsomeness. Ladies used to swoon, they say, in the course of his fine dramatic lectures. Robert Boyle too is an intriguing man with his long nose, sardonical air and flowing locks. He might be a rake or even a playwright perhaps; science is just another way of apprehending the world. Others have bushy eyebrows and pose with electromagnetic instruments.

I bought a postcard of Lord Kelvin from the gallery shop and wrote on the back of it: Please Explain The Theory Of The Aether. Love Penelope. Then I sent it to Sam.

It's not to be confused with ether, this theory. It's not at all the sort of stuff which came out of sinister glass bottles, patients etherized on tables, the magical substance which so eased Queen Victoria's confinements. It's far, far grander than that. Quite a grand illusion indeed.

Perhaps it was a mistake to send Sam my love. I don't think he needs it. More to the point, I don't believe that he wants it. Perhaps I should have sent my regards instead. Best wishes. I posted the postcard not far away from the Royal Opera Arcade. I didn't regret sending my love until Lord Kelvin went slipping through my fingers, plopping down into the red letterbox.

*

Passage from Smyrna to Constantinople. Sunday, August 19th.

At dawn Dickie joined me on deck. He was wearing a linen jacket with nothing whatsoever underneath it. His neck was muffled in a silk cravat. I, on the other hand, wore a frock of primrose yellow muslin with a good deal underneath. I felt gloriously fresh and sprightly. In my imagination, Mr. Nicolopulo's face kept re-appearing, smiling eyes and glossy beard. Dear Mr. Nicolopulo.

We paced up and down the deck. Now and again I had to take a bony pin and thrust my hair back into place.

On the western tip of the island of Mitylene there is a lighthouse. Its name is the Sigiri Lighthouse.

"Look Dickie, Gallipoli. Only think, Asia."

"Not Gallipoli, Addie dearest. It's Calipoli, you know."

Dickie's face has acquired a golden flush, rather like an ikon of the Russian church, a madonna of Smolensk perhaps. He was carrying a fat volume of autobiography. Dickie adores digging into the odd corners of human life, investigating the silly ways in which people go about their affairs.

I was tart.

"I never learned Greek. Miss Layard didn't go in for Greek. Neither did Mademoiselle Aimée. Even Papa drew the line at Greek for females."

"Such an acid tone. It doesn't become you, Addie. You're growing spinsterish, you know. Waspish. I expect poor old Rupert's had to tell you the truth by now."

I removed my veiled bonnet, shaking it sternly. It was unusual that Dickie should have sympathy for Rupert. Sympathy is not one of Dickie's virtues.

"I expect that you've known all along, haven't you?"

"I did try to warn you. An odd man, the Herr Professor. A most ingenious paradox."

"I do wish you wouldn't say Herr Professor. He isn't German."

"It's how I think of him, you see."

I did see. Just the same, I said: "You're not in the least interested in the truth."

"Oh no. Only in appearances. And with contradictions too. The best characters have the best contradictions."

And here, I am afraid, I did fail to keep a breath of sharpness from my voice.

"The truth is incidental, that's what you mean."

I remembered how Dickie had sketched my portrait

saying: "You are incidental." We are all incidental to Dickie's picture of the world. I am a woman without a past and my father is the Herr Professor. I do not know exactly what he makes of Rupert or Nettie Seawright or the indiscreet Doctor Banti.

"Do you know the story of how the Hellespont got its name, Addie?"

"No. And I don't think I want to. There's been an ample sufficiency of stories just lately. I've never relished the Greek ones. So unrealistic."

"It was named for a child dropped into the water. A very long time ago now. The child was called Helles."

"A daughter, I expect."

"Ah, Addie. How perspicacious you are."

Now I unfolded my panorama and began to study the scenery. Dickie pretended to read about the habits of a corrupt old General with a whiskery moustache. We were steaming by the plains of Troy. There were forests of valonia oak and the grand opening of the Dardanelles. On each side there was a fortress, one called Seddah Bahr and the other called Koum Kaleh. Their guns throw bullets of marble and granite. I was bolstering myself with facts so as to keep Dickie in his proper place.

"Did I tell you that I was to become a writer of gossip as soon as I reach Constantinople?"

No. Of course Dickie has not told me. Dickie says all sorts of things. They are not necessarily true.

"I thought you were to be Private Secretary to the Consul at Pera. Or was that just a story?"

"In addition to that, Addie. In addition."

"I can see that the two posts might be complementary."

Of course they might. With Dickie the left hand always knows what the right one is doing.

"I shall enter the employment of the *Levant Courier and Eastern Express*. I shall be obliged to compose my columns in French. Will you help me, Addie? You'll be amazed at the muck which I shall rake. People do confide in me, you know."

So they do. I don't know why I have never considered Dickie's talents in this light before. It is not as if he can be relied on to keep their secrets, though.

"And will you abandon diplomacy and gossip when Lady Fanny dies?"

"Every speck of it, Addie. You can depend on that."

"And in the meanwhile?"

I have always been partial to the word 'meanwhile'. Sometimes I drop it into the conversation, simply for the pleasure of hearing it. It suggests the passage of golden, agreeable hours. 'Meantime' has a harsher echo.

"I was thinking of calling myself Aladdin. Do you agree?"

But I was considering the case of Lady Fanny Addiscombe. When I met her, her hands were nothing but talons, liver-spotted too. Dickie's words were flowing gently past, a stream of minor chamber music. From time to time I imagined that I could hear Mr. Nicolopulo's voice, his words falling famously, one by one. Dickie's style of piano monologue is altogether different. One day I, too, would have liver-spotted hands.

"There's a black shadow crossing your face, Addie. Is it the Professor of Sanskrit? I shouldn't allow yourself to be distressed if I were you. You never know when old ladies are telling fibs."

By this time the fine haze of dawn had burned away and I was thinking of 'sans histoire', that lethal wasting disease. It must be very nice to spend your old age remembering your many charming lovers.

"Glad you're not entertaining the idea of that Murat Bey fellow though. Not your sort at all, if you don't mind my saying so. All right for a little tease like Nettie Seawright but for a sensible woman like you . . ."

"Now look here, Dickie. I don't have to put up with you, you know. I've told you before."

But Dickie was already pointing out that even the whiskered General's wife had indulged herself with a witty, dark-haired artillery Major. This blow had fallen upon the General while he was away at the Crimean War. Dickie wanted to read the passage which dramatized the moment of discovery aloud to me. Dickie adores prose which manages to be both discreet and revealing at one and the same time. Artillerymen, according to Dickie, are renowned for stealing the affections of other men's wives and firing carelessly upon their own infantry.

"You need a proper sort of chap. Nice and cuddly. That Greek perhaps. I'd give him a try if I were you."

I began to fold my panorama. I flapped it rather. Still, there was no avoiding Dickie's nosy gaze.

"I'm warning you, Dickie."

But Dickie never investigates a matter too closely. He prefers to drop a seed, allowing providence to water it.

"Over there, Addie. Do look. A boatload of crockery. And it's making for us, you know."

And so it was, a cargo of gilded cups and plates reflecting the light of the fierce sun. You could not describe it as a Mediterranean light though because we were steaming through the Sea of Marmora by that time.

"Dearest Addie, let me buy you a tall water jug. Then you will always remember this morning."

Dickie is very keen on memory. He holds that it is an art form in itself, which perhaps it is.

"I want a proper jug, not an incidental one. A cool and glossy jug, all my own."

Dickie laughed. He began rifling the pockets of his linen jacket for silver coins. Dickie is not in the least mean. It is just that he often goes out without any money, as rich people are prone to do.

"And what did Stavriti have to say?"

"Oh, Mr. Stavriti. They have Greek wine, you know, at the English Club and . . ."

For once Dickie was very business-like.

"Never mind all that. What did he advise?"

"He advised that there are English steamers which travel by way of Malta and Liverpool. They have treacle sponge on board. He thought that Rupert should book passage to England on one of them straightaway. He said that there was no use in going on."

Rupert of course is very fond of treacle pudding, toad-in-the-hole as well.

"No use whatever?" Dickie asked.

"He said that if Rupert persisted, demanded to see Grand Viziers and that sort of thing . . ."

"Well?"

"Then we would be dogged by dubious agents of the Porte. That was his very phrase. I asked Rupert most particularly. 'Dubious agents of the Porte', he said."

Dickie whistled. There was no use in considering whether Rupert would give up or not. Persistence is one of his qualities, I am afraid.

"He said that if there was to be any hope at all Rupert must behave like an arrogant brute who is as rich as Croesus. Turks are impressed by money, Mr. Stavriti says. We must have a splendid suite at the Summer Palace Hotel and millions of carriages. He also said that we should give a ball."

"Goodo," said Dickie, stacking up silver coins on the palm of his hand. "Grist to Aladdin's mill, I expect."

I was putting notebooks and charcoals into my muslin bag. When I was a girl I carried sheets of music in this bag, to and fro across Parker's Piece. It was nearly time for luncheon, our last on board the steamer.

"And now for your water jug," declared Dickie. "So that you don't forget."

It's wrapped in white tissue paper as I write, my tall

glossy water jug, folded in my second best evening dress. Not that I ever do forget things. I have a perfect memory.

*

The journey into Norfolk is famously difficult. It's kept that way, pour décourager les autres. Things have not changed much since Parson Woodforde's time. Tea on the train is horrible swill. If they feel so inclined the drivers bring the trains to a clanking halt at Shenfield or perhaps just outside Diss. If you complain too bitterly then they will tell you that somebody has thrown himself under the wheels of the train and that they are waiting to clear the body and scrub the track. It's all done in order to make you feel ashamed, to oblige you to bear up and take it like a man. They especially like to remind you that you have not paid for your seat at all, but only for the privilege of travelling on one of their trains. The A 11 too, is a monstrously inconvenient road, dangerous as well. There's a mist that comes down like the clappers in the hollows of the Thetford Forest. People quickly get bored of waiting behind lorries full of sugar beet, not to mention lumbering tractors. They overtake when they can't see a thing.

Just the same, the sight of your first pink-washed farmhouse is worth all the trouble. And I had taken rather a lot of books as companions for my journey. I was feeling distinctly flighty and effervescent at the thought of seeing Sam. After all these years he still kisses me, but he does it after the polite French fashion – a little frisson on either cheek. His voice is rather as Adelina has described Mr. Nicolopulo's, it definitely tickles your spine. I couldn't have drunk quantities of tea in any case.

Speaking of Sam though, I thought I saw him a week or two ago. I was getting off my underground train at Highbury, trying my best to arrange the books which I had borrowed from The London Library as the train roared out of the station on its way to Finsbury Park. I cannot describe the scent of the underground, I've often tried. It is a compound of grit and moisture and stiff, grubby overcoats, not simply new grime, but ancient grime too, a smell which was already established by the time people went sheltering from the Luftwaffe. In any case, there I was, breathing in this particular smell and trying to arrange my books. I looked up and there Sam was, glancing sternly at me out of a bleary underground window as if to say: "Come on then. Haven't you got yourself sorted out yet?"

My books were all to do with Adelina, books about the authenticity of diaries, books about Asia Minor and a volume of Murray's and the German *Baedeker* which she carried with her. I'm determined to track down copies of all the books which she wrote as well, though I'm still missing one or two volumes.

I don't imagine that it can have been Sam at all. He didn't smile or wave in my direction, which I think Sam would have done. He only appeared faintly aggravated by the muddle which I had made of my book bags (my favourite being my *New York Review of Books* bag, with Shakespeare's head outlined on it). My muddle used to aggravate him quite a lot if I remember properly.

But I don't mean to suggest that Sam had a dispiriting effect on me. That isn't why I asked to be divorced. He's far kinder and cleverer than Rupert Renishaw ever was, for example. In fact, reading about Rupert has made me realize how lucky I was. He used to make me laugh as well. I <u>don't</u> think that it was Sam. It was only a tall, dark-haired man with fine lines around his eyes. He even had threads of peppery grey in his hair, something which Sam cannot possibly have. When I first met Sam he was only twenty-four. He can't have grey hair by now. Even I don't have grey hairs yet.

I've found Adelina's postcard album with the

hand-tinted views of the ruins of the Temple of Diana and the white, cluttered harbour at Smyrna. It is made of watery green leather, the corners are bound in silver. It's a very grand postcard album, not at all the sort of thing which my mother used to buy for half a crown at village fêtes. I discovered it at the very bottom of the picnic hamper.

I keep remembering what Julia told me, about how writers write and don't leaf through picnic hampers. I wonder whether this is the only really useful piece of advice that Julia has ever given me?

I wonder if I should hand in my notice at Crick, Frick and get on with my life of Adelina? I haven't yet written of the *contretemps* which occurred after the office Christmas party. It's only my belief in telling the truth which makes me think that I should. The party was at the Dorchester, the men wore black tie. The thing is though, Marcus came home with me afterwards.

I took him home in a taxi. My next-door neighbour, Mrs. Munns, travelled up in the elevator with us. She was wearing an old silk evening coat with enormous round buttons. She took several long looks at Marcus. She sniffed meaningfully.

"Good night, Penelope. I only hope that you know what you are doing."

"Good night, Mrs. Munns. I only hope that Reginald is healthy."

Reginald is Mrs. Munns's cat. He lives in her flat and never sets foot out of doors. He has his own Edwardian bath chair.

"Of course he is," said Mrs. Munns sharply. "He eats nothing but Whiskas, you know. He has his claws manicured."

"Are you serious?" enquired Marcus, when I had turned the Chubb key in the door and hung up his coat.

Marcus was looking pink and healthy, full of brandy

and smoked salmon and duchesse potatoes. He's rather a treacle pudding type himself.

"Mmm, yes. At least, I think so. Where is Camilla?"

A black shadow swept like a cloud across Marcus's face. He was tearing off his bow tie, unlacing his shoes with astonishing celerity.

"Camilla is in the country. At the cottage. She hates London. Hates it when I work on Sundays. Hates it when I'm late home as well."

"I can understand that."

"Only wish I did. Never realized she *wanted* to see me. Thought the opposite as a matter of fact. Got a cell phone just so I could keep in touch. Because we see so little of each other, she buggers off altogether. Now we see nothing at all. D'you see the logic? I don't. The cottage has dry rot. And the chimney's collapsing. Not on the outside, mind you, on the inside. Much more serious. Eighteenth century irons left holding up the brickwork. No-one knows what to do about it. Have I told you this before?"

"Yes. At least I think so. You have to love old houses, you know. They're like people. Not worth the turmoil unless you love them."

By now Marcus was taking off his y-fronts, hopping from leg to leg. A familiar sight to Camilla, who once had loved him, and perhaps still did so.

What do they call it in *Fanny Hill*? That delicious stretcher? His unwieldy machine? It's a bad sign though when you're thinking about stories at a moment like this one. I could not help remembering that y-fronts were introduced into England in 1939. They came from America. Before that men like Marcus wore white boxer shorts.

"Can't seem to please her whatever I do," Marcus was grumbling.

"No."

"Never wanted to be the villain of her life."

"Of course you didn't."

I was still wearing midnight blue taffeta, ten denier stockings, French knickers and the rest of it. I grew up in an era when girls wore pants of the very skimpiest sort and no bras at all. It's very daunting to see underwear making such a comeback.

"Come along, Penelope. He who hesitates is lost. And we don't want to be lost, do we?"

"No, we don't. In fact, Marcus, the thing is . . ."

It was not simply the thought of Camilla. I was thinking of Sam when he was twenty-four years old.

"I don't like the sound of <u>that</u>. I'll unhook your stockings for you and you'll start to feel more like it. How lovely you smell. Sweet Penelope. Come along."

"The thing is, Marcus, I've made a mistake. A blunder. I'm most dreadfully sorry. I've changed my mind, I'm afraid. I am sorry. Truly."

Marcus blinked.

"You're cold, that's the thing. You're shivering. Let me warm you."

He was only a little crestfallen.

"Of course lots of chaps wouldn't take this lying down. They'd cut up rough, you do know that."

"I know. You're much too nice for that sort of thing though."

"D'you think so?"

"Of course I do."

Marcus smiled grimly, reaching for his y-fronts.

"In that case, dear girl, how about a brandy?"

*

August 19th. As I write it's late at night. Constantinople tomorrow. Domes, minarets and scented pleasures to come.

"Like a brandy?"

"Yes, please."

"I shall give you a peppermint before you go. Just to deceive your husband."

"He will not notice."

"Don't you think so?"

"No."

In the afternoon I went to visit Mrs. Seawright in her stateroom and this is how our conversation began. Mrs. Seawright's brandy was French, the very best, poured into sparkling balloons. Her enormous stout leg was propped on feather pillows. She was wearing a kimono of ocean green silk but her face was white as dough.

Nettie was absent, studying Greek with Mr. Nicolopulo on the boat deck. Mrs. Seawright does not want to deny Nettie the distinction of a proper classical education, simple Latin is not good enough for her own daughter.

"I do find that brandy is such a consolation, don't you?"

"I don't really know. When I was young I used to drink ginger wine with Mademoiselle Aimée in the cold weather. After skating."

Mrs. Seawright shuddered.

"Oh, my dear. Ginger wine. When you were young. Just as your palate was beginning to develop. What can your father have been thinking of?"

"Is the brandy a consolation to your ankle?"

"To everything, my dear. Absolutely everything."

I was beginning to understand perfectly. I sprinkled a little more into my glass.

Mrs. Seawright's portmanteau full of books stood in the middle of the floor. They were fat books, atlases and volumes of annotated texts. Mrs. Seawright explained that opinions were tedious, that facts were what were required in life.

"I'm only impressed by facts, you see."

I was glad to hear this because I had already decided that that was the sort of person she was. Some people adore opinions, others delight in facts. I have observed it often.

"Do let me sketch you. Portrait of a Lady With a Swollen Ankle."

Mrs. Seawright snorted. "Close the porthole, there's a good girl. I've got something to say. An opinion, I am afraid."

"Never mind. Fire away."

I can recommend brandy in the afternoon. It gives you a splendid assurance. I felt that I was quite prepared for anything.

Mrs. Seawright lifted her ankle thoughtfully. The ocean green kimono flapped. There was a deep frown on her face, serious business about to unfold.

"I shall need a cigarette. Hand me my box."

Mrs. Seawright waved the silver box in my direction. "Will you have one?"

"I never have before," I said doubtfully.

"What a lot you do deny yourself."

"It's because I'm afraid, I expect."

"When you begin to grow old the fear goes away. It simply disappears. You can't even remember what it was like to tremble all the time. The relief is wonderful."

This seemed perfectly logical, after all. There must be something worth getting old for.

"In that case I shall smoke a cigarette."

It combined perfectly with the heavenly brandy. I began to see my affairs in a rosier light. What was Mrs. Seawright going to tell me?

When her cigarette was lit Mrs. Seawright took a long puff and began.

"It seems to me that you are avoiding your husband. In my opinion that is a very bad policy indeed."

Everyone gives me their advice. Rupert and Dickie, Papa and Mrs. Bunn, now Mrs. Seawright. And I'm the most truthful and dependable one among them as it turns out.

"Oh no. I do not avoid him. I only aggravate his dyspepsia. And he likes to see me occupied."

"My father left me no money. Not a red cent. What about yours? Will he leave you a great deal?"

Tendrils of lavender smoke filled the stateroom. Her question was so unexpected that it took my breath away. Of course my father was not going to leave me any money. I don't suppose the thought has ever entered his mind. And now there was Mrs. Bunn to be considered, their child as well.

"My father is a Fabian Socialist. He does not believe in inherited riches. I expect he'll found a scholarship."

Mrs. Seawright inhaled deeply. What I had had to say confirmed her darkest fears. What with this and the matter of the ginger wine I could see that she was not developing an especially high regard for my father. This was a novel experience for me as most people admire him.

Evidently Mrs. Seawright was in the gravest of agony, not simply from her wrenched ankle but also from the knotted plummy veins in her calves. She kept rubbing her legs in a grave and absent-minded way.

Nevertheless, Mrs. Seawright applied herself sternly to my predicament.

"Fortunately my two husbands *did* believe in inheritance."

I agreed that this was an enormous stroke of luck. "But perhaps a woman should earn her own money? That is what Olive Schreiner advises."

Mrs. Seawright declared that earning your own money sounded quite effortless but turned out to be impossible. I think that she had heard of Olive Schreiner, a very strong-minded lady from Africa, but I cannot be perfectly certain about that.

"Believe you me, my dear. Impossible."

I am afraid that she pronounced 'impossible' after the French fashion – im-poss-ee-ble. It gave the word a more fatal ring than you might have thought. Very impossible indeed.

"Unless you have a talent for the writing of lascivious fiction, that is."

I did not confess that just lately I have detected just such a talent flowering within me, that I have even begun my own story of Balkan counts and abducted heiresses. It was not the sort of confession which would have interested Mrs. Seawright. I kept very quiet.

"A girl needs money. In short, she needs a husband."

I swallowed my brandy. I leapt to my feet. I was getting a little cross by this time.

"If you feel like that about it, dear Mrs. Seawright, you really should allow Nettie to marry her young man with a railroad. It would be the very best thing for her."

"In Nettie's case though, matters are differently arranged. Nettie will have a fortune of her own."

Yes, so she will. Why didn't I think of it? As gently as possible Mrs. Seawright was trying to tell me that I could not afford to indulge myself as she could with her stepson's tutor. I must think of my future and of keeping a roof over my head. I must behave sensibly.

I tried to suggest a way of changing the conversation, of nudging it a little in another direction. "It is Nettie's ambition to become a society hostess," I said.

At this news Mrs. Seawright's eyes narrowed. She lit another cigarette but did not offer me one this time. In any case I was on my way to the door, my hand was practically on the brass knob. It was very hard not tripping over the portmanteau full of books. I nearly stumbled over Schliemann's *Ilios*.

From far away there came the sound of a voice singing Alfredo's part from the beginning of *La Traviata*. Sweet Italian song lapped our ears. Mrs. Seawright appeared very thoughtful. I expect that she was weighing the qualities of all the society hostesses whom she had known, Mrs. O.H.P. Belmont and Lady Guernsey. I sipped the last vestiges of my lovely brandy. Apparently the Greek lesson was over.

Mr. Nicolopulo was singing *Misterioso!* and *Altero!* too. He was singing of joy and of love. Oh poor Violetta! What a dreadful mistake she made, giving up Alfredo like that. Sacrifice generally turns out to be nothing but cowardice in the end, doesn't it?

"Of course the part should be sung by a tenor," observed Mrs. Seawright. "A baritone simply will not do."

11.59 p.m.

As I was supposed to be dressing for dinner, I sat down in the middle of the floor to read *Amours de Voyage*. I had hoped that it might give me some ideas for my Balkan confection. I do this sort of thing all the time, it makes Rupert very stern because he believes that reading poetry is a sign of gloomy spirits. Naturally, reading poetry in the middle of the floor is even more shocking still. There are so many better things one might be doing, tidying up your stocking drawer or playing tennis.

Amours de Voyage is just like a novel, splendidly slim though. Clough makes it quite plain that love depends on accidents.

Rupert entered saying, "Poetry, ah."

I glanced severely at him. Then I carried on reading.

Naturally, I am not speaking to Rupert. That is because I'm angry with my father. This may sound illogical but really it's quite straightforward.

Still, I thought I should reply. The subject was not a personal one, after all.

"Literature does form your character, Rupert. Your ambitions too, you know."

For a second Rupert was quite nonplussed. He bent down to tie his bow tie in my speckled looking glass. His brow was crumpled in thought. He smelled of hair oil. He sucked in his breath, stroked his double chin.

"Dearest Adelina. I thought that cricket did that."

*

When I entered Sam's cottage from the narrow sloping street there was a cat in the middle of the sitting-room. She was clipping her toenails, making crunching, slashing noises, waiting for the fire to be lit. She was a proud and silky cat, not entirely displeased to see me, I thought. Her mouth was very wide and wicked, all the better to capture mice with. The house smelled faintly of damp plaster and wood smoke. It was very old and crooked.

I sprang across the little sitting-room.

"Jocasta!"

"No. Not Jocasta. Jocasta died of kidney disease. This is Antigone, her daughter."

Sam spoke with faint impatience. He began to strike a match for the fire. He had expected me to remember what had happened to Jocasta. Jocasta had been my own beloved cat and I had left Sam to nurse and bury her in her final illness.

It is in such situations that you realize that men are not all bad, that some are miles nicer than others. Far nicer than yourself, even.

"She is so very like Jocasta. The same in every way. She's lovely, isn't she?"

"Jocasta was a very promiscuous cat, if you remember. Antigone is far more discriminating."

I followed the line of thought suggested to me by the word 'promiscuous'.

"It's quite a prickly feeling being alone with you after all this time."

"I'd ignore that feeling if I were you. That's what I'm going to do. Most things go away if you ignore them for long enough. Later on we can talk about the aether."

The aether, yes of course. I had quite forgotten Professor Mackintosh's aether.

"After I've explored your house."

"There isn't a lot *to* explore, you know."

"I'd like to though."

I've got into the habit of turning other people's houses upside down, leafing through their letters and their photograph albums. It's more absorbing with live people than with dead ones because you can still get answers to all your questions if you are lucky and persistent. It's a logical extension of management consultancy, after all.

I found my bedroom right away. There were fragrant roses, a narrow bed, *Barchester Towers* to send me to sleep, even a carafe of water on my bedside table. Almost everything a person could want. Outside I could see a square of thick green grass surrounded by a holly hedge. Someone had raked together a heap of rosy apples and there were speckled starlings perched around the edge of a birdbath. They were leaping into the water, one after the other. Then they jumped out, shaking themselves dry on the edge. Starlings are not beautiful but they are very theatrical, companionable birds. You can watch them all day long if you have a mind to.

Now that I was upstairs I launched a search for evidence of other ladies. No traces in the bathroom. Nothing in my own room. No scented soap or paperback fiction. No honey and beeswax moisturizer. Sam is not secretive, just very discreet. I expect he would have told me all the details if I had asked him straight out. Perhaps he remembers how nosy I am.

When I went down again Sam was peeling cloves of garlic. He was very intent. When he had accomplished the peeling he began the crushing. The little kitchen was filled with the sharp scent of mangled garlic. I think that Sam was regretting my invitation. At the drop of a hat he can produce a splendidly absent-minded air which lets him out of normal conversation altogether.

"There's some wine. I think you'll like it. Antigone's gone hunting. She'll slither in later on, I expect."

"I have a neighbour called Mrs. Munns. She has a cat called Reginald. He gets his toenails clipped regularly."

"Well, good."

"Mrs. Munns interferes in my life. She says things in the elevator. In front of people too."

"Does she water your geraniums for you whenever you go away?"

"Mmm, she does."

"In that case . . ."

Naturally, it took me a long while to grow accustomed to Sam's narrative style, the pauses being so much more eloquent than the words. Sam grew up in the Mid-West where men are men and don't go in for a lot of chatter.

"Are you making something delicious for me? Sea trout and parsley butter, perhaps? Or Maryland crab cakes? In novels men are always making lovely, mouthwatering things. It doesn't happen so often in real life."

"The crabs are all gone. As for sea trout . . ."

He began chopping parsley with serene efficiency. I was reminded of Nettie Seawright bandaging her mother's ankle in Smyrna. Sam never cuts himself. I always do.

"It's chilli. I thought you'd like it. It's very hot. I put the red beans in to soak last night. I grew the peppers and tomatoes."

"You used to say that wine didn't go with chilli."

There was no point at all in expecting an answer to a statement of this sort. I made myself useful, I sliced the onions.

After dinner I investigated Sam's records and tapes and compact discs. Perhaps here was the evidence I was looking for. There were some very odd things – Fats Waller and *La Traviata*, *Iolanthe* and Buddy Holly.

"I saw Julia a little while ago," I said. "She's advising me about these Adelina papers."

"Julia?"

An indigo shadow danced across Sam's face. He got up to grind the coffee in an electric coffee grinder, a very noisy machine. I myself have always favoured coffee which is ground by hand.

Oh Julia, where are you living now? In the direction of Finsbury Park of course . . . Not far from my calm and tidy, blue-painted flat on the edge of Highbury Fields. Why didn't I think of it? And there are grey threads in Sam's hair now. I noticed them right away. I'm always looking for signs of decay in other people. It's a disgusting trait.

When Sam returned with the coffee he said, "About the aether. It was a thoroughly British idea. The notion persisted into the nineteen-twenties, you know."

"Yes. Carry on. Tell me the story of the aether."

I know that when Sam says "thoroughly British" he means inefficient and illogical, pompous too perhaps.

"It was thought that energy, electricity, in order to move about the world, must move in some element. As the tides exert their energy in water. That element was the aether."

"They made it up."

English poetry is full of the aether, you find it on every page.

"Of course they did. You can't smell it or see it. You certainly can't measure it. Nevertheless, in spite of all the evidence they believed in it."

Like God. Like love.

I found an Edith Piaf record, rather a scratchy one, in an old paper cover. Sam never used to enjoy Edith Piaf. I could make out little bits of it, here and there. I don't think Sam understands a word of French though. It's just mellifluous sound to him. He's not a linguist like Madame

Chrissavelonis. He wouldn't have been thinking of rosy pots of Lapsang tea or snowy afternoons, nothing like that. Sam does not believe in romance, only in happiness. It was a point on which we disagreed more than once.

"Quand il me prend dans ses bras, il me parle tout bas." My mother used to sing these words to me when I was a little girl, perhaps remembering snowy afternoons of her own. Before she went to London to interpret for the Poles, my mother was a radio mechanic at May Down in Northern Ireland, the only female in the outfit. I have a photograph of her kneeling in front of her aeroplane, a long time ago.

But of course that's all over now, il me parle tout bas and that sort of thing, not to mention my poor mother herself. She died of cancer of the breast two weeks before Adelina's notebooks were delivered to me.

When I asked her whether she had found a pea-shaped lump, she said, "No. There was no lump that I could detect at first. I felt a thorn being pressed into my left breast. Truth is stranger than fiction, you know. Doctor Osborne took no notice."

*

August 20th. Constantinople.

As we disembarked at the Golden Horn, Dickie waved in the direction of Scutari, a jumble on the Asian shore, where there was once a British military hospital. I am afraid that Dickie is one of those gentlemen who cannot help smirking at the mere thought of Miss Florence Nightingale.

"There, Addie. What you've come for, I expect."

I took out my opera glasses and held them to my face.

"Not exactly, Dickie. Not altogether."

Doctor Banti came to say goodbye to me. Rupert sniffed. Doctor Banti bowed. He kissed my hand.

"Such tiny hands, Madame. So unnaturally pale."

"I am English, Dottore. We are all unnaturally pale."

"So you are. How could I forget? You must visit me at Buyukdere. We shall have a picnic, yes?"

"I would love to."

A mysterious veiled lady came to meet Doctor Banti. They say that he has two wives, one in Marseilles and one in Constantinople. How lucky men are. What tidy arrangements they are able to make.

We went by steamer to Therapia, on the European shore. Dickie got out his Murray and began pointing out the mosques and villages and palaces to me. The wooden houses were painted all the colours of the rainbow. There were marble quaysides and landing places with ornamental gateways. The water was of the deepest blue.

"Look Dickie, the wonderful colours. I've never seen anything like them."

"Yes, Addie. I'm glad that they make you so happy."

In the east of England all colours are water colours. There is nothing like this. There the earth, the sea and the sky are nothing but variations upon one another. Here they are quite separate. At Rumili Hissar the architecture of the castle spells out the name of Muhammad, the letter M being represented in a series of fine sturdy towers.

"I shall paint the castle," I said happily. "I shall do it in oils."

"Oh, Addie. Abandoning charcoal and watercolours. It's unpatriotic. Whatever next?"

"I have sent a postcard to my father. To Professor and Mrs. Mackintosh."

"Ah!"

"Remember what Kitty said about men who say 'Ah!'"

"I do. I never forget it."

In loud tones, Dickie proclaimed: "'Therapia deserves its name from the salubrity of the air: for the cool winds which blow directly from the Black Sea, temper the heat of the summer and render it one of the most charming residences on the whole of the Bosphorus'."

"Thank you for reading to me."

"And before you go, I've got something for you. A tiny present, nothing grand."

It was wrapped in scarlet tissue paper.

"I don't like giving you another book. You have far too many of them as it is. They are such a bad influence. Still."

"Thank you."

"Do stop thanking me. Unwrap it, Addie. Come along."

"But you've already given me a beautiful jug."

"I like giving presents. It's one of my nicest traits. Unwrap it. I do hope you'll like it."

I unwrapped the scarlet parcel. *The Letters of Lady Mary Wortley Montague*. The book smelled of roses and leather binding, the cabins of the steamer too.

"Oh, Dickie. Thank you. I shall begin to-night. I shall love it, I know."

"Now, now, no fuss. A little keepsake to cheer you up. You must lend me *Amours de Voyage* in return."

I shall not see Dickie so often now. The Ambassador's summer residence is at Therapia but Dickie will be gone at Pera a good deal of the time, busy collecting useful information and drafting peremptory telegrams. I waved goodbye to him at the quayside. I was very sad to see him driving away in his fly.

"Come along," grumbled Rupert. "I'm looking forward to a decent breakfast at last. Bacon and eggs. Kedgeree. Toast. Get a move on."

The last page in my second notebook. Will the third notebook last for the rest of my journey, I wonder?

PART THREE

*The Summer
Palace Hotel*

Therapia, The Summer Palace Hotel. August 20th.

As I turn the pages of my journal I cannot help noticing that I am growing quite lazy about times and dates. I carry my journals about with me all the time now so that I can write down anything which enters my head. The only trouble with this is that it disrupts the smooth flow of events so that instead of becoming a story my diary becomes like daily life itself, nothing but a series of episodes with no proper ending to them.

This morning Rupert said, "I can't say that I like the way that you're always sitting about writing nowadays."

This took me by surprise. I did not think that he had noticed.

"Can't you?" I replied.

"No. It's quite unnerving. Are you writing about me?"

"Sometimes. Not very often. Would you like it if I did?"

Rupert was counting his boiled shirts. They smelled of Parisian steam and starch. He has brought his winter vests with him to Turkey, spats too. Rupert has always been very particular about his clothes, he knows exactly how long a shirt cuff should be, and what sort of braces are the most gentlemanly.

"Therapia means cure, you know," Rupert harrumphed, slamming shut the last drawer of a tall and stately mahogany chest.

But I do not require curing. Or do I?

"You should be playing tennis instead. Tennis is wonderful for the circulation of the blood. You would sleep so much more soundly if you had an energetic game of tennis in the afternoon."

"Do you think so?"

"Of course I do."

Thanks to Dickie I know now that Therapia was not always called Therapia but that once it was known as Pharmakia or 'poisoning' after the poison which the Goddess Medea scattered along the Thracian coast. Did I mention that it was very grand here? It puts the Hotel Oriental in Marseilles to shame. There are a lot of German visitors too, here for the fishing, and they are renowned for going where the service is best.

"There. Finished at last."

Rupert glanced at himself in the looking glass, brushing an invisible speck of dust from his shoulders.

"Do you think that I should get my hair cut?"

If I had married Walter Ramage I would have known all about Maxwell's equations by now or even the motion of particles rather than the rise and fall of treacherous stocks and shares. Walter, though, has not forgotten me. Three weeks ago he accompanied me to a cricket match at Fenner's. The air smelled of cut grass and Cambridgeshire rain. I clapped gently; Walter perused *The Times*. We drank champagne and munched a veal pie which was baked in the kitchen of Walter's college. Walter filled our glasses without spilling a single bubble. It is not that Walter speaks very much when we are together. He does not. He is rather silent. He likes me nearby, that is all there is to it. He thinks that I am a nice person to share a bottle of wine with. I could not help leaning back in my canvas chair, closing my eyes and thinking: "This is what it would be like if I had married Walter."

*

"I can't remember," said Julia. "Was I invited to your wedding?"

"I didn't have a wedding, Julia. At least not one you could invite people to."

I was very humble. Both Julia's weddings were splendid affairs, with a display of sumptuous presents and mouthwatering caviar, not to mention tiny bridesmaids got up as fairy princesses and a string quartet.

"I always fancied Sam."

"I know you did. It doesn't matter now. I don't think that he would have gone in for the sort of wedding that you enjoy."

"I saw him a little while ago, actually."

"Please don't say anything more. It's nothing to do with me, you see."

Julia and I were lunching at one of my favourite restaurants. It is in the cellar of a tall pretty white-painted London house. There are pink damask cloths on the table and vases of spiky, scented parsley. Julia was nibbling a spinach salad with a dressing of walnut and stilton. I was digging into moules à la crème.

"You shouldn't eat so much cream, Penelope. You'll get fat."

"I am fat, Julia. I don't mind."

"Of course you mind. What piffle. There's nothing worse than fat."

"There are lots of things worse than fat."

"Do you think so?"

"I do."

"Of course, your mother was very stout before she died."

Stout is a horrid word, a horrid drink too. When she was young my mother was beautiful, just like Anna Neagle. A slender stalk of loveliness. There is evidence that she outdid Julia at every turn. I remember her especially in a suit of heather-coloured tweed, pure nineteen-fifties

Chanel. Remembering that suit I hear the voice of Edith Piaf singing *Autumn Leaves*. My mother had a skin of a delicacy which no amount of money will buy for you.

"The thing is, Penelope, you're all right as you are now, soft and voluptuous, but you mustn't allow it to get out of hand."

"I'm like a painting, I'm lovely," I said stoutly.

I dipped my bread into my cream sauce. I like delicious, distinguished food. There were fragments of garlic glistening in my sauce. At the next table a man and a woman sat in consummate silence. I envied them. Julia was busy crunching on a walnut.

"My mother had a very romantic wedding. It was in 1947. The lavatory was frozen. My father wore his Polish uniform. The wedding feast began with carp, just like a Polish Christmas."

"Oh, the winter of 1947. Do you think that they made it up?"

Julia wriggled on her uncomfortable little bistro chair. It was not simply that 1947 was far too far away to be imagined, it was also far too icy to be imagined.

"No, it definitely happened. I've seen the evidence. My mother wore thermal underwear beneath her wedding dress. Long johns."

Julia wrinkled her brow. Her forehead is broad and creamy, her eyes a clear, discommoding periwinkle blue. She can give you the feeling that you are in a *viva* and that things are definitely not going your way.

"Weren't they ticklish, her long johns?"

"I don't know. I never asked her."

My mother and I did not speak of bodies, not even ticklish long johns. That was part of our agreement.

"You should have done. It's the flavour of an event which counts. You should remember that when you write about Adelina. It's far better to say 'her knickers were scratchy' than it is to give a blow by blow account of the history of underwear."

"Do you think so?"

"Of course I do."

"Granny was just like you though. She had masses of weddings, all very comme-il-faut."

Julia looked pale and injured.

"You can be so horrid."

"So can you. Now where were we?"

"There's something I came to say. I thought it would be kind to tell you."

"Tell me then."

"Pudding first?"

"I like cheese best. Vignotte. I've got my wine to finish, you see."

"Oh, Penelope."

"And what about you? Profiteroles?"

"Well, perhaps. They are so delicious, aren't they?"

I had to wait for my cheese while Julia ate her pudding, it's that sort of place. In the end they brought minute cups of sharp aromatic coffee. I drank mine gratefully.

"Did I mention that I'd seen Sam?"

"Did I mention that I didn't want to hear about it?"

"Oh no, Penelope. Nothing like that."

Julia widened her eyes. She has no wrinkles. She does not lie awake at night wondering whether she has done the right thing.

"Mmm, well. It's nothing to do with me."

"Oh, but it is, Penny. I'll tell you why."

"Why?"

I did despise myself. What weakness. And it's not as if you can rely on Julia's judgement. It isn't in the least sound.

"Because he still loves you, Penelope."

"Did he tell you this, Julia?"

"No. No, of course he didn't. He doesn't talk a great deal. I knew, that's all. A person like me knows these things. I was a psychological social worker, remember. I'm not entirely stupid."

"No-one was suggesting that you were stupid, Julia. Just wrong."

"I'm telling you. He loves you."

He loves me. He loves me not. As far as I can see people have not stopped falling in love but they have stopped <u>loving</u> one another. He loves me not is by far the safer of the two assumptions.

I asked for a Calvados. Julia winced. It came in a brandy balloon, golden nectar with a powerful scent. I could not help remembering how Granny went to bed and died with a glass of Calvados at her side. Much more sensible than bothering with an ambulance.

"You're not listening to me."

"Oh, but I am. You're wrong, that's all."

"He loves you."

"He doesn't. Even Antigone doesn't like me."

Julia said: "Who is Antigone?"

"Sam's cat," I replied. "She's his cat."

*

Tuesday August 21st.

I have spent the entire afternoon at work on my delightful melodrama. The story is coming along nicely, there are even moments when I can feel it fizzing in my blood. This is what has happened so far:

Having escaped from the vicious stepfather who is determined to consign her to a loveless marriage with the mysterious Sir Piers Vicary, my fictional Nettie has been captured by Turkish pirates in the Mediterranean. Naturally the captain of the pirates has grown exceedingly fond of the made-up Nettie. He reads poetry to her and tells her the story of his adventurous life as he draws upon an endless stream of intoxicating cigars. This debonair captain speaks no English, only French and Turkish so that they are obliged to exchange melting glances and long sweet sighs. By now my Nettie character is struggling with her dictionary, longing to tell the captain of the pirates the story of her astonishingly <u>un</u>adventurous life with her noble, saintly mother and wicked Rumelian stepfather, there being nothing like a love affair to make a girl diligent in the study of her foreign languages.

In the meanwhile my heroine's stepfather, the Balkan count, has dispatched emissaries from his palace in Sofia. They are searching for my fictional Nettie, enquiring everywhere they go. I remember what Dickie once said about the best characters having the best contradictions so that while my heroine is herself a very noble girl she is distinctly susceptible to the charms of the captain of the pirates. At night, as her head lies on her pillow, as she turns and tosses in the sultry heat, she dreams of her pirate captain, her mouth waters for him, she smells the scent of his cigars on her long silky hair and she longs to feel his arms enclosing her . . .

Yes, yes that's exactly what I am after, sultry heat and intoxicating cigars, long melting glances and sweet sudden sighs. In Ouida even the most sensible of heroines suffer from deadly faintness. I think I shall oblige her to keep a journal. At every entry she will weaken, drawing nearer to her seduction. The question is, will it be the pirate captain? And what about Sir Piers Vicary? And why has her mother turned out gentle and saintly, a thing which in my observation true mothers very seldom are?

*

After my lunch with Julia, I came home and uncorked a bottle of Chinon wine, Clos de l'Echo as a matter of fact. Usually I'm very happy to unlock my front door and step into the hallway of my little flat. I like coming home, running an eye along my shelves of books, smelling my flowers, pouring a boiling bath. Tonight though, the flat seemed empty and frightening, as though it belonged to some strange person with curious tastes. That is why I decided on the Clos de l'Echo. Wine is definitely a consolation, Mrs. Seawright was perfectly correct.

A long time ago now Sam and I visited Chinon. We stayed in a hotel beside the Vienne. You could hear the splutting of vélos together with the lapping of the river in the depths of the night. That summer there was a breath of the past in the air, the dusty longue durée. There were shuttered windows, the paint flaking gently away. Our bed was fine and high, a bed of nineteenth century proportions with a starched linen bolster. It was made of warm red wood, burnished wood, cherry, I think. Early in the morning we were awakened by the smell of buttery croissants baking gently in an old steam oven. In those days we were still in love. At nights Sam would take me in his arms and sing to me: "Words of love you-ou whisper soft and true, darling I love you."

But Sam is not in love with me now, of course. I was far too unkind to him for there to be any danger of that. Still, the notion that he might be has been discouraging me from work all day long. Adelina's journals are lying forlornly on my wooden kitchen table and I am supposed to be writing a report about an airline reservation system which is perpetually breaking down. It's costing somebody millions of pounds every day but I don't appear to mind at all. Why should I? I'm thinking of abandoning air travel altogether it has grown so sinister and disgusting. I remember once at O'Hare Airport . . .

Never mind about O'Hare. Let's stick to the critical path here. What did Adelina say about gentle and saintly mothers? That there were no such things? It's time I said something about my own mother, the girl who got married in long johns in the winter of 1947. She's becoming a shadowy figure, as the mother of the diariest is apt to be.

In the first place she was devoted to Sam. She found it difficult to put up with me after we parted. She was of the opinion that a good man is hard to find and that once you find one you should stick to him. In the second place . . . Well, the second place will just have to wait for the moment. There's someone ringing wildly at my front door.

*

August 22nd. Morning. Stamboul.

A portrait in words: Lovely Nettie bargaining in the bazaar.

I shall not describe the bazaar. Every visitor to Stamboul writes a lapidary account of the bazaar. Even my celebrated Vicomte counsels the reading of Théophile Gautier and refuses a description on his own account. He does tell you how to bargain though, most useful advice. Mrs. Elliot, my other authority, scorns any mention of the famous bazaar but does give an affecting account of the pariah dogs of Constantinople.

Mrs. Seawright did not join us for our expedition to the bazaar. She remained in her suite, drinking mineral water, brandy and sweet Turkish coffee. The swelling in her ankle has reduced but now Mrs. Seawright is subject to a curious lethargy and shortness of breath. Last night I went to see her and we drank brandy together and smoked her cigarettes from the silver box.

"Have you sent for Doctor Banti?" I enquired of Nettie as we set out for the bazaar in our smelly fly.

"Of course not," said Nettie firmly. "He is a charlatan. I have sent for a proper American doctor."

In the absence of her mother Nettie is growing firm and decisive. She wears her emerald ring every day now; she has begun to draw the name of her lover into every conversation so that now I know which operas he likes best and which novels too. His name is Newton Schuyler and Nettie loves him because he is perfectly proper, not in the least singular or foreign. Some girls do adore men who are thoroughly reliable, others are the very opposite. In this respect the real Nettie and my fictional heroine have already begun to diverge. It all depends upon your upbringing. The véritable Nettie has quite forgotten the remote and black-haired Mr. Murat Bey, a man who is a past master at bargaining, I expect.

This morning we visited the rug market. Mr. Nicolopulo walked between us, anxious to protect us from villains and urchins. He would far rather have taken us to an improving museum, he does not in the least approve of the wicked merchants of the bazaar.

"Oh, I shan't pay that," Nettie declared. "I wouldn't dream of it. What robbers they are! Tell him that I shall pay half, Mr. Nicolopulo. Not a lira more. Mr. Grimwade, my trustee, is very strict. He invites me to lunch once every year in order to urge me never to spend money if I can avoid it."

I have decided that Nettie must be the daughter of the Chicago meat packer after all. It is not as if she requires the Vicomte's good offices. Nettie was born to bargain and seize her own way.

"Will you buy a rug, Mrs. Renishaw?"

"I don't need a Turkish rug just at present, Nettie."

Mr. Nicolopulo, who plainly detests bargaining, obeys Nettie's instructions to the letter. Whenever he is obliged to be more peremptory than usual his cheeks flush and his fingers tremble ever so slightly. I keep a close watch out for his gentleness, his sorrowful clever eyes.

"Everyone requires a Turkish rug, don't you think?"

Like all the very rich people whom I have known, Nettie has a very pronounced idea of what it is that everybody needs. She admires the little silk rugs best, as who would not? Her lips part as she studies them. She cannot resist touching them, a fingertip here, a thumb there. They are far too beautiful ever to step upon. Even in the gloaming of the bazaar their colours dance and glimmer. Perhaps I should purchase a rug for my father and Mrs. Bunn, a belated wedding present?

"Oh no. I've got quite a lot of them already."

And that is true. Old Mr. Renishaw gathered a fine collection of oriental treasures. Our house is filled with magnificently glowing carpets, from Persia and the borders of China as well as Turkey. Even if this were not the case, there is no money to buy Turkish rugs just at the moment.

When she had made elaborate preparations for her rugs to be transported to the Summer Palace Hotel, Nettie made a dash in the direction of another stall. As she ran, her little chain mail purse flapped, her silky hair went flying.

"Oh, look. Slippers, how lovely. Who can I buy slippers for? I know, you. Not Mama. Her feet are too swollen for little slippers like these. It will have to be you, Mrs. Renishaw. Come along now. Aren't they heavenly? Try something on."

The slippers were soft as Parisian gloves. They had pointed toes and were inset with morsels of mirror and slivers of stained glass.

"You must, you must. I'm not to be thwarted."

Mr. Nicolopulo pointed out that the slippers would not be useful in the English rain, that they would shrink and crack, the pieces of mirror would tumble out, that they might appear cheap but that truly . . .

"NOT TO BE THWARTED," exclaimed Nettie, choosing a pair of slippers which were embroidered with silvery thread and decorated with glass of rosy amethyst and blood-red garnet.

"Here you are. These are the ones," Nettie insisted.

"What a very generous girl you are, Nettie."

"I am exercising my will," said Nettie. "I don't think that that should be confused with generosity, do you?"

No, no of course not. I inclined my head. I conceded the argument.

Soon we were strolling in the direction of the spice market. There you will find rosewater, henna, cinnamon and vanilla, opium, tobacco and Persian hashish. I was thinking of my heroine, about to be sold into a Turkish harem. I can see her face but I do not know her name. At first I thought that it was Henrietta but now I know that her name is not Henrietta at all. It is something simpler, something far more poetic than Henrietta.

I ventured so far as to squeeze Mr. N.'s shoulder. He fixed me with his brown eyes. No-one else appeared to notice. I expect that the dragomen of Constantinople are perfectly accustomed to the attentions of voracious English ladies.

"Is it true, Mr. Nicolopulo, that you can buy a woman in Constantinople?"

Poor Mr. Nicolopulo was deeply mortified. Like Mr. Murat Bey he would rather pretend that Turkey is a European country, whereas in fact, it is the very opposite. I do not think he understood why I should pose such a sharp question, coming as it did so soon after the squeezing of his shoulder.

"I am a Christian, Madame. I know nothing of these matters. They are conducted in secret. But it is true, yes. You may buy whatever you like in the bazaar of Stamboul."

Thoughtfully, Mr. Nicolopulo was rubbing the pattern of fine lines which are to be found above the bridge of his nose. His eyes were watery with embarrassment. He cannot know that I only tease him because I would much rather throw my arms around his neck and hug him very tightly.

128

"They do say, Madame, that educated women command the highest prices."

Yes, I expect they do. Useless things are always more expensive, aren't they? Think of the little silk prayer rugs upon which you must never tread.

"In that case," said Nettie, "I shall abandon Greek altogether."

"Oh, Nettie. And you were just beginning to master it."

"No, I was not. Mr. Nicolopulo will tell you. I'm an atrocious pupil. I won't even agree to the alphabet. I am lazy and disputatious. Mr. Nicolopulo says that these are the two worst faults that a person can have."

"Not the worst faults that a *person* can have, Mademoiselle," Mr. Nicolopulo demurred softly. "Not at all. They are the worst faults that a *pupil* may have."

Disputatious is a word which Nettie must have borrowed from Mr. Nicolopulo. I have observed that he has a weakness for solemn words and elaborate pictures.

Mr. N.'s face was a picture of – what shall I say? – sagacious gloom. I do not suppose that he can afford to lose a pupil as rich and distinguished as Nettie is.

"There is no dearth of intelligence, Mademoiselle. It is the will which is absent, I fear."

I expect that he must mean the will to learn Greek. It is not as if Nettie were wanting in any other sort of will, after all.

*

The fierce ringing at my doorbell was Mrs. Munns, wearing a grey cashmere cardigan and short fur-lined suede boots. She was brandishing a fat envelope.

"The wrong address. Just look at this."

"I'm very sorry, Mrs. Munns. What can I say?"

"You know that postmen can't read," she said accusingly.

But who can read? It's a vanishing art, everyone agrees.

"Never mind, Mrs. Munns. You're very kind to bring it to me. I expect that it's rubbish, you shouldn't have bothered. Do you remember the days when people got real letters?"

"I still get them," boasted Mrs. Munns, her eyes glittering. "I have one daughter who lives in Brazil and another who lives in Ross and Cromarty. They are both very sparing when it comes to telephone bills. I don't suppose you've got any liquid paraffin? Reginald's got a hair ball."

"Would cod liver oil be any good? I've got some of that."

"Mmm. I could try. I used to give cod liver oil to my children. Susanna would tip it down the lavatory. I'm glad we don't get hair balls, aren't you?"

"Is Susanna the daughter who lives in Brazil?"

"No. Susanna is the one who lives in Ross and Cromarty."

I invited Mrs. Munns to drink some wine with me, I told her that I had just opened a bottle.

"Certainly not. I can hear my programme coming on. I do hope that this cod liver oil of yours works."

Mrs. Munns returned to her flat, locking the front door several times behind her. I too could hear the sound of her programme beginning.

A brown envelope, posted in Kent. What might it be? It doesn't matter though. I poured myself another glass of the Clos de l'Echo and stuffed the envelope away in the drawer of Adelina's canterbury, one of the few pieces of furniture which I have brought here from the Cambridge house. I've brought lots of chamberpots and soup tureens though, they're excellent for planting bulbs. Mostly I don't like furniture. I like bare painted walls, wooden floors and bowls of scented flowers. I like household smells, polish made of beeswax and turpentine, vivid brown Dettol and melting onions. I can't sit here describing smells though, I've got to get on with Adelina. Julia expects it. She is waiting for my first chapter.

I've looked up the reference to Mrs. Elliot's pariah dogs. They roamed all of Constantinople. They were troubled by yellow suppurating sores and were pitifully thin. Mrs. Elliot naturally found them more affecting than the hungry children who roamed the city. Even so, I'm not entirely persuaded that I think the less of her for that. You can only do one thing at a time. This notion that it's only people who count is quite wrong in my opinion. Someone ought to defend the ladies of the nineteenth century, high-minded, energetic and blessed with such enigmatic papas as they were.

But I was going to tell about my mother, wasn't I? I've been putting if off. Adelina has become a character to me, Granny too. But my mother is not a character. She refuses to become one. She is my sine qua non instead. My grandmother has danced with Sergeant Eiselbe, pulled on her gloves and introduced me to Mary Queen of Scots, so that I would know a silly woman when I met one, and to the young Queen Victoria, so that I would grow up to be dutiful but not unworldly. My great-grandmother has of course presided every step of the way. I really had hoped that now that she's dead my mother might have relented, consenting to become a character, a girl of the nineteen-forties, just as Great-Grandmama was a Victorian and Granny a ragtime girl. Just the same, it hasn't happened. In my head she still speaks out of turn; she's still amorphous. She was my mother, the person who used to say: "I am your Mother." She is the one who still reminds me that I am nobody's mother. I've only got the one picture of her nineteen-forties girlhood. I'll get out my magnifying glass and give it a good look.

There she is, my mother. She is eighteen years old, the

photograph was taken in Northern Ireland. The year was 1943. She was just about to meet my father, Felix, who was at least seven years older than she was.

At first glance, peering through a magnifying glass, the details swim before your eyes. You lose your judgement, your way. Then matters begin to fall into place, the picture begins to reveal its secrets. What is she wearing? A white shirt and naval bell-bottoms. A navy blue jacket of clean lines. She is not wearing the tricorne hat so admired by Colonel Hevingham because she was not a petty officer. At the time of the photograph my mother was a Leading Wren. She sits cross-legged in the front row, she's making a daisy chain, I think. Behind her there are rows of muscular chaps, their sleeves rolled up for action. My mother is smiling too, the happiest, prettiest girl in the picture. She was a radio mechanic and I treasure this picture because it was taken before she was my mother. A few weeks afterwards my father, Felix, flew into her life. Her outfit maintained the planes for a training unit. The unit specialized in night flying, the Lorentz beam approach. Felix, a blue-eyed and melancholy hero of the Battle of Britain, was on a refresher course.

Does any of this help? No, of course not. It would be far easier to just make her up. Stories are what help you to understand the world; it is the truth which is mysterious and intractable.

The last time I saw my mother she was lying in bed, apricot-coloured liquid travelling by tube into her chest. Chemotherapy, as is well known, has little effect on cancer of the breast. My mother was brave, just like a heroine of the Second World War. She said: "This is not the worst thing that can happen to you. You can bear this as well as I can. You can believe me because I am your mother."

Now that she is no longer around to correct my version

of her life she will perhaps begin to assume the proportions of a character. I do hope so.

Her name was Penelope, just like mine.

*

August 22nd. Wednesday afternoon.

As I was taking a bath in my magnificent bathroom, sliding up and down in the scented water, I was visited by the certain knowledge that my heroine's name is Maude Grey. Maude Arabella Grey, as a matter of fact. I do not quite know how Maude's virtuous mother came to marry the unscrupulous Rumelian count but that does not signify just at the moment. In stories of this sort the first principle is that something must be happening all the while, it need not be anything which is either likely or logical. With a name like Maude no-one will suppose that my heroine is a baggage at any rate. They will expect her to be a noble girl, full of rectitude. They will sympathize with her temptations.

My bath stands on claw feet of brass. There are marble tiles on the floor, creamy ones and black ones, too. Once Rupert would have come into the bathroom for a chat with me, not nowadays. Instead he is composing letters next door. Tomorrow morning he has appointments to attend to while Nettie, Mr. Nicolopulo and I are to inspect the Museum of Antiquities. I think that Mrs. Seawright must be growing worse and worse: the American doctor has forbidden all visits and at luncheon poor Nettie's face was wreathed in anxious frowns. Whatever will she do if her mother dies here in Stamboul? Will she send for Mr. Newton Schuyler?

*

There it is. Mariora Chrissavelonis. Maude Grey. Silver grey. Mariora Silver. You don't need a PhD. to figure that one out, do you? And to think that I can't even get my first chapter written. She wrote dozens of books. Is this Freud's fault? Is it to do with entropy? Is the universe simply running down? I do things, after all. I get up before Farming Today comes on the radio. I go to meetings. I write reports. I'm a whiz at presentations and I've earned lots of money. Nothing to show for it though. No letters. No diaries. No tea chests full of fat leatherbound books.

What gave Adelina so much energy all of a sudden?

Getting rid of poor old Rupert, I'm afraid.

I write 'poor old Rupert' because I've begun to feel sorry for him. I know what has caused this sudden attack of sympathy. It's knowing that he is going to have a heart attack and die very soon, that his wife will abandon him and his business collapse. It's a shame to see Rupert crumbling. He used to sail so confidently through life, now look at him. He twitches and splutters, loses his temper and his shirt studs as well. He can't even make up his mind whether he needs a haircut or not.

Is this Adelina's fault? Not entirely, not altogether. It is the world which wears you down – other people, husbands especially, are nothing but the agents of your fate. From the very beginning though it's been plain that Rupert bores her, a lethal weakness in any tapestry of affection. I do remember that in the opening pages of this notebook I used the word 'ennui', didn't I?

I don't think that Adelina would have enjoyed it if he <u>had</u> come into the bathroom for a chat. Whenever Adelina enters a room, you are aware of her eyes darting in the direction of the remoter corners. Across a crowded room Adelina is looking for a stranger, a man who will make her laugh and see the world freshly. That is what love is, after all.

*

Our flies were reserved for ten o'clock in the morning. Nettie took breakfast in her suite and when she came down she was no longer wearing white but lilac muslin instead. Her anxiety of yesterday is a little assuaged; Mrs. Seawright slept deeply in the night, only waking twice in the turgid, wet heat and this morning she has eaten a softly boiled egg.

The important thing about the day though was this – Mr. Nicolopulo kissed me in the garden of the seraglio. He tasted, yes, <u>tasted</u>, of cigars – just as I once imagined that Mr. Murat Bey would do. I have a horrid feeling that it was all my fault, that I stepped into his arms and lifted my face to be kissed and that in all gentlemanliness he could not have resisted. To resist would have been to make a drama and Mr. Nicolopulo is by nature a gentle and undramatic man. When our kiss was ended there was an unaccountable expression in his brown eyes. Was it, perhaps, apprehension? I do so hope not.

I cannot say exactly what happened the rest of the day. My heart kept on beating, but very loudly. I am surprised that nobody heard it. I felt dangerously faint. I glided through the famous Hall of Bronzes without seeing a thing.

"Dear Mrs. Renishaw," said Nettie as we were stepping into our conveyance once again. "You are looking very pink. I think that we should drive to Pera and treat ourselves to a citron pressé, don't you?"

I said, "What a splendid idea, Nettie."

Mr. Nicolopulo drank iced coffee. Nettie ordered a cream cake for herself and ate it very greedily, the crumbs cascading down her lilac muslin.

"And now I shall have another," she declared when the very last mouthful had disappeared.

I must say that it was quite unnerving to see Nettie gobbling down her cream cakes. For a moment it even made me forget the kiss in the garden. I wonder whether Nettie has been indulging in midnight feasts all along? Only the cynical Mr. Murat Bey might have predicted this turn of affairs. He always imagined Nettie as a young lady capable of action and calculation.

"Won't you have one?"

"No. I couldn't possibly."

"More to drink?"

"Mmmm."

When Mr. N. absented himself Nettie lost no time in asking me whether I had enjoyed my visit to the museum.

"Of course I did. I loved every minute."

"Mr. Nicolopulo is amazingly quiet, don't you think so?"

"Yes, no. That is . . ." I mumbled.

My citron pressé was very soothing. All the same, it did not do a great deal to restore my powers of thought.

"Generally he likes to talk."

"I expect that it was the heat of the afternoon, you know, Nettie. It turns some people to gin, others to silence."

"He only looks at you."

"Rubbish, Nettie."

"And when you dropped your glove . . ."

Oh, the dropping of that glove. I have not described it. It was an accident. I would not go so far as to deliberately drop a glove. I am not half-witted; at least, not yet. Still, there is no doubt that love makes you behave in all sorts of foolish ways, everyone is agreed upon that.

"Tell me, Nettie. Were you _ever_ in love with Mr. Murat Bey?"

Nettie laughed with delight. Shavings of ice tinkled in her glass. Her gooseberry eyes were very bright. It is lovely to see her munching and chattering.

"I managed that episode amazingly well, don't you agree?"

Naturally, I <u>was</u> obliged to agree with her.

"When I met him in Heidelberg I thought that he might be useful to me in my battle with Mama," Nettie said shamelessly. "But I am going to marry Newton. No-one else will do for me, you see."

Ah, Newton. What fine words. No-one else will do for her. A young man with light hair and a railroad all of his own. Stern eyes, though. I wonder if Nettie has noticed? Yes, I expect she has. Nettie is such a sensible, hard-headed girl.

I think that she was seriously considering the prospect of a third cream cake when she caught sight of Mr. Nicolopulo in his black straw hat, weaving his way through the tables as he returned to us.

"I do like him, don't you?"

But how could I not like him? He listens when I speak and smiles so very warmly. There are those, after all, who gaze upon one with cold, positively jellied eyes.

"Of course I do."

"Has he shown you a picture of Madame Nicolopulo?"

"No."

I do not wish any ill to Madame Nicolopulo, you see. It is simply that I wish that she would vanish in a puff of smoke.

"I expect that she is very fat with jowly cheeks and thick wrinkles across her forehead, don't you think so?" asked Nettie, with infinite kindness.

"Oh no. I expect that she is very beautiful, that she sings like a nightingale and that her eyes are black and dreamy. At least, that is how I have pictured her. Generally speaking, you know, people do turn out to be as you have imagined them."

"Do they?" Nettie's eyes widened in wonder. "Really?"

"Of course they do."

*

But how much does all this owe to Mudie's Circulating Library? And how will I ever know? Anyone who could write about great quivering sighs could easily have made up this stuff about kisses in gardens.

When Adelina died she left her notebooks to Dickie Ricardo with instructions that they were to come to me one day. This was odd because Dickie was already dying and Adelina knew it. I expect that she did not want Granny to read her journals but there she did Granny an injustice. Granny was not interested in other people's lives. She liked her own life best of all, never mind anyone else's. She would never have read the little leatherbound notebooks, much less would she have torn them up and thrown them away. Granny was a firm believer in allowing people their privacy. Just the same, they went to Dickie who deposited them at his bank. At the bank the notebooks got lost, along with Dickie's birth certificate and some of his great-aunt Lady Fanny's worthless Russian mining shares. A little while ago the bank discovered them and sent them to me. The shares were to be mine, Dickie said so, and I have decided to have them ceremoniously framed. In any case, that is how I came by Adelina's notebooks.

I wish that I had found them in a tea chest in the attic like the Mariora Silver novels. I would like to know that they had been lying there untouched for nearly a century. As it is, I know that Adelina had until 1959 to edit her diaries and that afterwards Dickie took them.

I had a phone call at work today. I was getting on with my report about the airline reservation system, clicking away at my Macintosh. Marcus claims that the entire difficulty is nothing but a technical muddle. Poor old Marcus is losing his grip, his tie is always loose nowadays and sometimes he even wears brown socks with his pin-striped suit. I've heard no news of the management buy-out lately; even his wife Camilla has forgotten

Marcus, she never rings to say that she has lost her keys, never rings at all in fact.

Victoria strode in the direction of the telephone, snatched it up sharply and shouted, "Good morning. Crick, Frick."

Victoria has abandoned the leather clothes which once upon a time so delighted old Mr. Crick. Now she wears pencil-straight skirts and extravagantly soft Italian sweaters. No navy blue suits for Victoria. Just lately Marcus has arranged a promotion for her. She has become an administrative assistant and is above answering our telephone. We have Rosalind to do that for us now.

"It's for you. An estate agent in Cambridge."

A nice estate agent, very pukka. Victoria was dimpling.

"You must speak to them, Penny. They're very impatient. They've called you before."

"Right."

I held the telephone to my ear, hoping that Victoria would go away, which she did not.

"Miss Katanowska?"

"Yes?"

"We've got some news for you. We hope you'll be pleased."

"Go on then. Tell me all about it."

Someone has made an offer for Professor Mackintosh's house. I felt an instant of remorse, a shiver skipping down my backbone. I had grown used to the idea that no-one would ever want it. The leaky roof and the rotten banisters have been frightening people away. The thing is though, I haven't got much time left. All that mould to be sponged away, all those tea chests to be emptied.

"The buyers are rather impatient, you see. I wouldn't hesitate if I were you. Could you move out by November the 15th?"

I explained that I had been rummaging through the attic, that there was quite a lot of stuff up there, a good deal of scrubbing to be done too.

"Did you tell them that the house once belonged to a famous lady?"

But of course, Adelina is not famous. No-one remembers her travel books. No-one has heard of Mariora Silver. It is up to me to make certain that people have heard of Adelina. I shall do the best I can.

"I'll do the best I can. November the 15th it is."

Victoria was agreeably impressed. She is fond of property and appearances, though not in exactly the same way as Granny was. The very suggestion of money lends quite a lilt to her voice.

"Are you going to be very rich?" she enquired.

*

3.00 a.m. August 24th. Summer Palace Hotel. Written in Mrs. Seawright's bed chamber.

"Monsieur, Madame. You must open your door at once. It is an emergency. Un cas d'urgence. A matter of life and death."

"I'll go," I said. It was not as though I had been asleep.

"No," groaned Rupert. He squirmed among his linen sheets, emerging on the other side of the wrought-iron bed.

"It's my job to go to the door in the middle of the night. That's what husbands are for."

One of the things, at any rate.

Un cas d'urgence.

"I expect it's Mrs. Seawright."

"I shouldn't be at all surprised. I'd go back to sleep if I were you. I shall take care of everything."

I am afraid that Rupert was enjoying the idea of taking care of everything. He was hurrying into his spotted dressing-gown and leather slippers.

"Oh no, you won't. I'm coming too."

Rupert shrugged. "Put something on your feet then, Addie. Those things that Nettie gave you."

In the half-light, the coloured glass in my new pair of slippers winked and blinked, the silver thread shone; they were like magic slippers in a fairy story.

"I shan't be a moment."

"Good."

Rupert was unlocking the door.

"Come along. You don't need that notebook, do you?"

"You never know. I might. Navy blue ink too."

"Good God!"

Rupert's slippers went padding along the marble corridors of the Summer Palace Hotel, my little slippers went swishing along.

"Come along, Rupert. She'll be dead before we get there."

Rupert sighed gloomily, tightening the belt of his spotted dressing-gown.

In Mrs. Seawright's suite we found Dr. Banti mixing a potion at the marble nightstand. He was wearing an old velvet coat, patched at the elbows.

"Here they are," said Mrs. Seawright. "So glad that you could come."

"Chère Madame," said Dr. Banti, turning away from his collection of powders and packets. "Such a pleasure."

"How lovely to see you, Dottore. Let me kiss you."

"No, no. I shall kiss you."

We kissed; Rupert frowned, eyeing Mrs. Seawright's glowing brandy bottle. He does not believe in all this unnecessary kissing. Gently, Nettie fanned her mother's face with a fan made of sandalwood, the scent drifted through the high cool chamber.

As I kissed Doctor Banti, I could not help thinking of the veiled lady who had come to meet him at the harbour. Why do women so adore this bright-eyed little man? Because of the sympathy in his expression, I think, and the way in which he inclines himself in your direction. I expect that a great many ladies have told him their secrets.

Mrs. Seawright began pouring.

"I can't do without Dr. Banti's powders so he had to come here. He is so very kind. Nettie sent a telegram this morning."

The dottore smiled at me over the top of his spectacles, knowing what I was thinking.

"Ah," I said. "So that's where you went to, Nettie." Nettie blushed.

"We are just waiting for the card table," Mrs. Seawright explained.

Nettie was fluttering at the bedside, plumping up pillows, scattering droplets of eau-de-cologne, patting the linen sheets. Mrs. Seawright's voice was deep and resounding. Even so, you could tell that she was very weak. One side of her face appeared rather stiff and her skin was the colour of faded old parchment. Was it a stroke? Yes, I think so. It is what old Mr. Renishaw died of – though he died at home on a horsehair sofa like Emily Brontë, not in a grand and foreign hotel.

"I have sent for sandwiches," Mrs. Seawright reassured everyone.

"And what about us?" Rupert harrumphed.

I have begun to notice that one way or another Rupert is always saying "What about me?".

"You won't mind having a game of whist, will you? And will you drink some brandy? French, of course. Not Greek."

I opened my notebook and settled into a chintz-covered armchair. There was a knock at the door, the sandwiches arriving on a brass tray.

"Breast of smoked turkey?"

Mrs. Seawright inspected the sandwiches, even going so far as to peer inside them. Just the same, her voice possessed an iron timbre so that I knew immediately that no-one would dare to defy her.

"Or would you rather salade de poisson? I expect that you've noticed the first-rate mayonnaise that they provide here. The worst thing about being ill is having your appetite melt away altogether. Food has always been such a comfort to me when things were at their worst."

"I shall partner Mrs. Seawright," said Doctor Banti. "You, Signor, must play with the young lady."

"Shouldn't we cut for partners?"

Rupert is always a stickler for things of this sort.

"Oh, my dear fellow, no. Not necessary at all. Have a sandwich."

Mrs. Seawright was wearing her ocean green kimono, sipping her brandy, studying Rupert. In the shimmering light her eyes appeared narrow and stern, as though she were looking at him through a telescope. Poor Rupert, I felt sorry for him. Just the same, it is a very bad omen, suddenly beginning to feel sorry for your husband after so many years. What was she about to say?

"Someone else is joining us tomorrow."

Rupert's mouth was overflowing with turkey sandwich; he was not bothering to return her attentive glance. Nettie tripped across the room to take him his brandy.

"Yes?"

"I have received a letter."

I do not think that Rupert knew what was coming; I did though. Rupert was caught with his mouth open.

"It was from Madame Chrissavelonis. She is arriving by steamer tomorrow from Smyrna. With Flora McPhee and the two little girls."

Rupert stopped munching right away. He put down his turkey sandwich and gulped his brandy. There was no mistaking his pleasure. If we had been alone together and properly dressed he would have been whistling and jingling the coins in his pockets. As it was he turned very rosy, just like a boy.

"We shall look forward to that, shan't we, Adelina?"

"Yes, indeed."

I expect that Rupert does find Madame Chrissavelonis very soothing, her methods being so entirely different from my own. It is astonishing how gentlemen do discover that other people's wives are just the ticket. But perhaps, he does not find her soothing at all. Perhaps he finds her just the opposite. Even so, I do not think that he should presume too far. She did once say that she believed in turning the tables on men, after all.

Another knocking at the door, this time it was the card table.

"Over there, over there." Doctor Banti waved his arms excitedly.

"You will play, won't you?" Mrs. Seawright commanded. "Another sandwich? Salade de poisson this time?"

Obediently, Rupert helped himself to another enormous sandwich.

I wrapped my feet in one of Mrs. Seawright's tartan blankets.

"You won't need that," Rupert advised loftily.

"I'd like it though. We get cold feet in my family."

Doctor Banti smiled, stirring his potion with a long silver spoon.

"For Signora Seawright."

"Thank you." Mrs. Seawright sipped the doctor's thick white mixture, grimaced and hauled herself from her high-backed mahogany bed. "My American doctor never gave me anything like this."

"That is because Doctor Faulkner is a proper doctor, Mama."

The poor dottore looked rather injured by what Nettie had had to say. Mrs. Seawright grumbled, "Now don't scold me, there's a good girl."

144

Nettie ran to put an arm around her mother.

"Come along now. Let me."

"No, no. I can manage without you." Mrs. Seawright became peevish, thrusting her aside.

They arranged themselves around the table. I remembered the game which had taken place on board the steamer, the shadows cast by the light of the oil lamp. I took up my pen, swallowed my brandy and began to write of how Maude, running breathless through the jasmine-scented garden of the seraglio, stopped only to throw her jewelled slippers into the cool and sparkling fountain.

But where is she going? What will become of her?

I don't know, I don't know. I expect that it will all become crystally clear to me before very long. I do hope so. I am waiting for a flight of fancy.

As she ran she heard the frenzied baying of the hounds in her wake, the clacking of the painted wooden shutters as they were flung open to the night air, the plashing of the water in the ancient fountain. They were after her now . . .

"My very last game of cards," said Mrs. Seawright contentedly.

*

What a lot of questions she does ask. I do wish that she knew more of the answers. Wisdom is what we expect from our great-grandmothers, after all, not more questions. It's very odd to think that I have only to walk over to one of my white-painted bookshelves in order to discover what became of the virtuous Maude Arabella. I found a copy of that particular book in the depths of the tea chest. It's entitled *The Lady from the Seraglio*. I wonder what <u>will</u> happen to her? What always happens to virtuous heroines, I suppose.

I'm tempted to record the time, as Adelina does. In any

case, it's the very middle of the night. In the vicinity of three o'clock. I couldn't sleep at all and while I was busy not sleeping, wriggling my toes and turning over my pillows, I remembered the fat brown paper envelope which Mrs. Munns brought for me the other evening. As soon as I remembered the envelope, I turned on my light, jumped out of bed, and hurried into the sitting-room. Where was it? I wondered. Oh yes, in the canterbury.

I tugged at the narrow drawer, pulled out the envelope and ripped it open.

Inside there were two black and white photographs. Attached to the photographs by means of a gold paper clip there was a printed business card.

With the compliments of Colonel Hector Hevingham.

From Colonel Hevingham. So the colonel's name is Hector. How very strange. I wondered why Colonel Hevingham had suddenly decided to send me a packet of photographs. They were modern photographs too, nothing whatever to do with Rupert or Adelina or the Ottoman loan.

The photographs were of a collection of elderly gentlemen dining together. They were healthy, bright-eyed old men, seated at a very long table, a forest of glasses spread in front of them. They were not wearing paper hats but the pictures lent that impression: paper hats, jokes, speeches, cigars. Some of the old gentlemen were wearing burnished medals. One was pounding the long table with his elegant soup spoon, another was affectionately thumping the shoulder of the tubby white-haired man seated beside him. No-one was glancing impatiently at his watch. Along the table there stood tall bottles of vodka. I polished up my useful magnifying glass. What sort of vodka was it?

Then I noticed that one of the gentlemen had caught Colonel Hevingham's special attention. He was a handsome old man with thick lustrous hair swept back from his face and glittering eyes. He was smiling over the top of his gold-rimmed spectacles, telling a story which was causing everyone to double up with laughter. There was an asterisk faintly pencilled beside his head.

"Is this your father? I remembered your name, you see. I thought that he might like to have the picture. Perhaps he's already got a copy, I don't know. Anyway, here it is. Reunion dinner. Very drunken occasion. Got a report on it from one of my old friends. I've still got my spies, you see. How's your Ottoman loan stuff coming along? Have you consulted the archivist at the Baltic Exchange?"

But how can it be my father? My father ran away to Poland and we never heard from him again. We waved goodbye to him at Victoria Station, he was travelling via Paris. When she got home from the station, my mother discovered a letter hidden underneath her pillow explaining that he would never return.

My dear Penelope, our life together is over. I shall return to my homeland. We will never meet again. Fondest wishes, Felix.

That is what he wrote. A fine mélange of the pompous and the melodramatic. Not at all the sort of character of whom Mrs. Seawright would have approved. Later, when my mother had recovered her pride, she caused his letter to be framed in a silver frame and hung upon her bedroom wall. When I asked her why it was there, she only laughed, dabbed a spot of Chanel on the inside of her wrists, and said, "Lest we should forget, darling. That's all." And on another occasion, when I had asked what sort of man Felix had been, she said, "He was a man who suffered from hideous nightmares."

"Of the war?" I asked.

"Of Poland," she replied, adding that he had had a lovely voice, full of gloom and Chopin.

Colonel Hevingham has run across someone else with the same name, that's all there is to it. There's no other explanation.

All the same, I haven't been able to go back to sleep. I

think that I will make myself a pot of soothing camomile tea, perhaps even fill my pink hot water bottle. How is it that I've spent all this time delving into Adelina's life and never wondered about my own father? I'll take *The Lady from the Seraglio* to bed with me. I am sure that it's very soporific and anyway it's time that I began to read the Mariora Silver novels. In addition to singing *Autumn Leaves* and *Il me parle tout bas*, I cannot quite help remembering that my mother was fond of telling me how truth was stranger than fiction. I wonder if that is going to turn out to be the case, after all?

*

The same day. 10.00 a.m. Friday.

This morning there was a letter from Dickie saying that he would show me the finest forest in Turkey, Lady Mary Wortley Montague's house too. He enclosed a scandalous piece of writing about the German Ambassador's mistress, the first of Aladdin's concoctions, which he expects me to put into French for him. I would have got out my Larousse and begun straightaway but there were two other letters for me, one from my dear friend, Walter, the other from Mr. Nicolopulo.

I was drinking from a little apricot-coloured cup with a golden rim, a cup of English porcelain so fine that you could read a newspaper through it. Rupert was drinking bitter coffee, munching his croissants.

"You look pale," said Rupert. "You'd better drink your chocolate. Lucky you can swan in bed all day. I've got to see the Grand Vizier. No good expecting you to sympathize. I'd give your hair a good brushing, if I were you. It looks like rats' tails."

"Shall we have lunch together? Perhaps at the Russian café in Pera?"

The sunlight was streaming in. Another grilling day about to begin. I thought for a moment of cold Ely Cathedral, thin droplets of Fenland rain. Rupert was very respectably dressed, he smelled of barber's lotions and unguents. I was wearing one of my Paris negligées.

Rupert gave me a quick, sharp, dry, little kiss on the cheek.

"Shan't want any lunch. Drank too much brandy in the night. Goodbye then."

He was jingling the coins in his pockets, whistling too. It must be the thought of Madame Chrissavelonis's arrival. I do not seem to mind at all. I wonder whyever not? And Rupert is quite mistaken when he says that I do not sympathize with him. I do. I wonder how he will proceed with her, how she will respond. I am amazingly sympathetic altogether. I do rather hope though, that they get it over with quickly.

Standing at the mirror, tweaking his moustache, Rupert said, "A letter from that scoundrel, Dickie?"

"Do you recognize his handwriting?"

"Mmm. Been seeing it for years now."

"Do you mind?"

"Never thought about it. Doesn't do to think too much about the likes of Dickie Ricardo."

"Perhaps not. Will you be going soon?"

"I must drink my coffee first."

"I would if I were you."

Rupert tossed back the last steaming particles. It is extraordinary how little there is to say nowadays.

I thought that perhaps Rupert would mention my hair again before he left but he did not. I believe that the thought did cross his mind. I saw him press his lips together.

"Au revoir."

"Goodbye, Rupert."

Dickie has invited me to drink tea and raki with him at a

café in the Forest of Belgrad. Afterwards, we will view
Lady Mary's villa. Walter, well, Walter just wants to
make sure that I have not forgotten him. But that's pre-
posterous, how could I forget Walter, the man with the
kindest, cleverest eyes in all the world? As for Mr. Nicolopulo, he writes that he would like me to read the chapters
of his Constantinople book and criticize them for him. His
words are written in black ink, stern and upright and true.

"I know that you will give me your honest opinion, Madame."

Of course I shall. Giving my honest opinion is a particular failing of mine.

I replied, *Come tomorrow. Come in the afternoon. Drink tea
with me, Mr. Nicolopulo.*

I could not help remembering what Mrs. Seawright,
in healthier days, had told me about the pleasures of
love in the afternoon, followed by draughts of re-
vivifying tea.

*

I was sitting calmly at my desk perusing *Webster's Dictionary* when the phone began to ring. I stole my copy of
Webster's from Sam on the night when I packed my case
and left home forever. It is especially useful for synonyms
and antonyms.

"You get it," said Victoria sternly. "Rosalind is still at
lunch, you know."

I took up my fountain pen, ready to take notes.

Julia? My estate agent? Sam, perhaps?

No, none of the above.

It was Camilla Monckton-Smith, Marcus's wife. Her
voice is very Penelope Keith-ish, the sort of voice which is
instantly obeyed on every continent, a voice which meets
no obstacle in splintering diamonds. Just the same, there
is definitely something to be said for ladies like Camilla.
They do not fuss. Nor do they whinge.

"Marcus has spilled the beans about the two of you," she said. "You needn't worry about me. I shan't stand in your way. I just wanted you to know."

"Camilla, you see, I . . ."

Why can't I ever think of the proper thing to say at the proper moment? My tongue felt dry and white and furry.

"Never explain, never apologize. In any case, I'm not sure that I mind desperately. Of course we don't have divorces in my family and I do feel a little numb. Just the same . . ."

I had the distinct feeling that Camilla had dressed up specially in order to make her telephone call. I had a strong impression of tweed suit, steam-pressed silk shirt and spanking new lipstick. She sounded very determined. Beneath her brisk words there lurked a hint of pure pleasure, absolute self-indulgence.

"I shall keep the cottage in Suffolk, you can have Marcus. You're very welcome. I've just had a damp course put in, you know. It makes all the difference. But Marcus must be responsible for the school fees. I shan't feel guilty. I know all about those weekends in Paris, slap-up dinners at Prunier's, Lucas Carton and the rest. Those starlit walks in the Champs de Mars. Marcus was very frank."

I felt a resurgence of innocence, I'd got my tongue back by now.

"What's this all about, Camilla? I certainly haven't been having any weekends in Paris. My grandmother took me to Prunier's when I was a girl. Since then . . ."

"Come along now, Penelope. I've given you my terms. If you want Marcus you can have him. I've got my trust fund, you know. I can afford to be generous. Good thing, actually. Repairing the chimney won't be cheap. I shall have to find an expert. Let's just try to be grown up about this."

"Now wait a moment, Camilla. There's something I've got to tell you . . ."

"Don't let's give him time to change his mind, Penelope. Strike while the iron is hot. No shilly-shallying."

"Camilla I . . ."

"I'm putting the phone down now, Penelope. I'm on my way to my solicitor's."

"The thing is . . ."

No good though. She slammed the phone down. It buzzed angrily in my ear. What was I supposed to do next? Find Marcus? Ring her back?

Victoria, who had been skimming *Hambros Performance Rankings Guide* while listening nosily to what I had to say, started crossing and uncrossing her long legs. She wears very extravagant stockings, fine and silky. They glint even in the grim, daffodil light of our second storey office.

Down below us British Gas was excavating the road, drilling away as best they could. Before their arrival it had been British Telecom. They have an agreement, first one, then the other. They haven't a breath of compunction about it. A taxi was stopping, old Mr. Frick was slithering out, carrying a pair of muddy waders, two packets of Marks and Spencer's sandwiches and a long-necked bottle of pink stuff, rosé de Provence, I think.

For a moment, I floundered. What was to be done? Then it came to me, as sometimes things do. I must leave the office immediately. Start on Chapter Two. Stop frittering my life away. It was suddenly all very clear. It isn't failure which is to be feared the most, it's not trying at all which is by far the more shameful.

"If anyone wants to know where I am, Victoria, please tell them that I've gone home."

Victoria appeared rather flustered. Her lovely blue eyes were moist and tender. I expect that she is the girl who has been enjoying the gourmet weekends in Paris, the midnight strolls in the shadow of the Tour Eiffel. I do hope that she doesn't abandon poor old Marcus altogether, he is the sort of man who does so require a wife, someone to organize his French cuffed shirts, compose his Christmas cards for him and keep his wine glasses properly gleaming.

"When will you be returning?" enquired Victoria with high formality.

I began slapping things into my leather bag, *Webster's*, skinny fountain pen, the *Financial Times*.

By now Victoria was growing plaintive, as though it were all my fault.

"I do have to be able to say something, don't I?"

She began stretching for my engagement diary, flipping through all those pages which are so full of lunches with people whom I do not like, meetings where no breath of a decision is apt to be taken.

"I'm not in the least sure. Never perhaps. Tomorrow I'm going to Cambridge. I shall catch the train, I think. I'll let you know."

I had taken two steps out of the door when I decided to go back and give Victoria the benefit of my wonderful advice. I was visited by the memory of other occasions, real and imaginary, when I had not said what I longed to say. All that's behind me now though. I am not in the least afraid of seeming bossy and meddling. After all, it's not just people like Camilla and Mrs. Munns who should be allowed the many delights of self-indulgence.

"I'd make up my mind quickly if I were you, Victoria. Then stick to it. No shilly-shallying."

As I said these words, Camilla's words, Victoria's face turned white and woebegone. I could tell that she shied away from the notion of taking Marcus under her wing, bringing him comfort and protection.

"Of course I must consider Marcus's happiness, mustn't I?" she said solemnly.

"Well, that's the question, don't you think so? Do you really want to consider Marcus's happiness for the rest of your life?"

Victoria turned paler still.

"It was your own pride I was thinking of especially. And the management buy-out, of course. There's a lot of money involved, you know. Money's not to be sneezed at, you'd be the first to agree. You don't want to distract Marcus unnecessarily, do you?"

"No, no of course I don't."

The mere mention of money had brightened dear Victoria. She began leafing through her *Hambros* once again.

"Just keep it in mind, won't you?"

"Yes, yes I shall. What a lot you know. You're very wise, aren't you?"

I only wish that more people thought so. I only wish that it were true. I'm working on it though, going for it, as you might say.

*

Evening. Friday 25th.

When Rupert returned his face was white and stiff, the wings of his hair limp and damp.

"There's nothing for it," said Rupert, bracing his shoulders. "We shall have to sell our house, there's nothing else for it. I shall make other arrangements, don't worry. You won't mind, will you? You have never liked it."

It did not seem a sensible idea to answer this accusation right away. Instead I went and tugged at the bell. Rupert paced up and down, one of his black shoes squeaking on the wooden floor.

"I shall send for some refreshing white wine. We'll have a drink. Olives and bread too. I expect that you are hungry."

"They didn't even give me coffee. I waited five hours."

By now Rupert's face had changed from stiff and white

to pink and squashy. I felt very sorry for him. Not to be given coffee is the gravest of insults, Dickie has told me so.

"I'm so sorry. Let me hug you. Things will get better. They always do."

"Not now," said Rupert. "I've got to see to my accounts. I hope you realize that we are quite penniless."

Fortunately, I did not marry Rupert for his money. What canny girls his sisters, Kitty, Lucy, Letty and Marie, turned out to be, keeping their fortune in three per cent Consols. The collapse of Renishaw and Vignier will not disturb them in the slightest. They can carry on just as before with tea parties, games of whist and indolent glassy-eyed cats perched on top of the green baize. How very astute of them. I wonder what might have happened if the girls had had the business and Rupert the Consols? Would matters have turned out very differently, do you suppose?

*

As I was coming in from Cambridge this afternoon, shaking my umbrella, I came across Mrs. Munns in the downstairs hall. Her face was grim, her wrinkles appeared to have deepened and her eyelids were swollen and puffy. She was carrying Reginald in a very grand picnic hamper. It had thick worn leather straps, tightly buckled. A series of grisly yowls was escaping from the hamper, a good deal of scratching and hissing too.

"Now, now, Reginald. Mother's here."

"How nice to see you both. How are you? What a lovely basket."

"Hand-made in Great Yarmouth," said Mrs. Munns. "A very long time ago. They specialize in baskets for hot air balloons nowadays. My husband Bill was exceedingly fond of picnics. Cricket picnics, I should say. Pimms and cold chicken for the scorching days. Flasks of whisky and mulligatawny soup for the rainy ones."

"It's beautiful, isn't it? First-rate for Reginald."

All of a sudden, Mrs. Munns's eyes filled with tears. I rang the bell for the lift. She dabbed at her eyes with a pink paper handkerchief. Reginald had turned alarmingly silent. I could see his green eyes glaring out of the picnic basket.

"It wasn't a hair ball after all. It was an obstruction. There's not very much that they can do. Reginald is coming home from his operation."

Words like obstruction, polyp, lump make my blood run cold. I'm a coward, there's no use trying to mask it.

"Oh, Mrs. Munns. Poor Reginald. What hideous news. Whatever can I do to help?"

"Nothing, my dear. Absolutely nothing. He has such a splendid vet. They think of everything. They explain it all. Far kinder than when Bill . . ."

I had not known that Mrs. Munns's husband was called Bill. I remembered that she had a daughter named Susanna who had been prone to empty her cod liver oil into the lavatory pan.

I imagined Bill tall and gruff, a sarcastic barrister or a headmaster who had once taught mathematics, a rapper of knuckles, a tweaker of ears. But perhaps I was entirely wrong. Perhaps he was a quiet, cuddly man of the sort who is forever murmuring "Whatever you say, my dear, whatever you think best."

"Vets are far nicer than doctors. Better at their jobs too, I think. And much cleverer. Please come upstairs and have a drink with me."

Mrs. Munns nodded.

"Not wine. Whisky please. Not a smoky one. Sainsbury's would be perfectly all right."

"Whatever you would like. I've got a lovely, velvety malt. Speyside malt, not smoky at all. It was a Christmas present, I've been saving it up."

"I'm sorry to be so gruff. I mustn't break down, you see. Nobody would understand. He's only a cat."

The lift in our building is very old, people get stuck in it all the time. It wheezes and shudders.

"Come along. Let's step inside and hope for the best. Get Reginald upstairs and pour our drink."

"Splendid. Thank you. And he might pull through. You never know your luck. They wouldn't rule it out altogether."

By now Reginald was scuffling in his hamper, whimpering to be let out. I don't think that animals know that they have to die. I do hope not.

"Let's unstrap this, shall we? You hang on to him, I'll carry the hamper. I've been far fonder of my cats than most of the people I've known."

"No comparison is there?" said Mrs. Munns. "People are so much trouble, so little comfort."

In the afternoon I had visited the Whipple Museum which is to be found in a winding grey Cambridge street. I peered at brass orreries from the eighteenth century, burnished telescopes and polished wind pumps. I thought of Rupert and Adelina, Nettie and Mr. Newton Schuyler, Mrs. Seawright and her two husbands, Professor Mackintosh and Mrs. Bunn. I thought of Sam because it was he who first took me to the Whipple Museum. It's rather a hushed and unfrequented museum, perfect for feeling sad in on a rainy afternoon.

As I was leaving the museum I bought a postcard. At the station I wrote on it: My Dear Sam, Have you ever heard of a man called Walter Ramage? Where can I find out about him? Love, Penelope.

The poles of the lamps at Cambridge Station are painted pillar-box red now, the bricks of the station buildings, once a dismal black, are scrubbed and honey-coloured. I might so easily have bought a ticket for the train which goes north to Kings Lynn. It was a wonderful evening for the journey across the Fens, fingers of rosy cloud in the sky, mist on the horizon, a breath of frost waiting to descend on the fields intended for beet and turnip.

Just the same, I did nothing of the kind. Instead I searched my canvas shoulder bag, my raincoat pockets too, and in the end I found my railway ticket. It was marking my place in *The Lady from the Seraglio*. I'm getting on now, more than halfway through. I took a window seat and began to read. The intrepid Maude Arabella – got up in a caftan of rose damask, embroidered with bands of silver flowers – was hurrying breathlessly in the direction of the port, hoping to encounter a steamer on the brink of sailing for England. But what did she find? Nothing but a dark-haired and taciturn Englishman who tells her only that his name is Sir Peter and that he is the owner of a gloomy estate in Lincolnshire, inherited from his mad cousin, Lady Blanche Vicary. Even a pea-brained girl like Maude Arabella might have suspected that this was the man that her stepfather had arranged for her to marry against her will. Even so:

"And will you help me, Sir Peter?"

"If it lies within my power, I shall. You must trust me entirely. Come with me now."

"I cannot wear my caftan. No captain would dare take a Turkish lady on board his ship."

"There will be no difficulty in that direction."

"No difficulty, why, Sir Peter . . ."

"There must be no delay. Time is not on our side, dear Maude."

"You are so very kind. How shall I ever repay you?"

"This is no time to speak of recompense, my dear young lady. You must come with me at once. Take my arm."

"But tell me, Sir Peter. Where are we going?"

"Now that I have found you, Maude – I may call you Maude, may I not? I shall take you . . ."

His grip tightened upon her arm; he inclined his dark face in her direction. In that moment it seemed to Maude that a diabolical languor was creeping over her, as if she could struggle no longer against her fate, as if . . .

"I shall take you to your stepfather, my dear young lady. I must not fail in my duty. I must take you now. This very moment."

"My stepfather, the wicked Rumelian count, oh Sir Peter, I beg of you . . ."

*

Tea with Dickie. Saturday August 26th.

The afternoon was sticky, there were thick grey clouds. Dickie drank raki; I drank lemon tea. Dickie was in fine fettle, I waited to find out why.

"Did you read my piece about the German Ambassador's mistress?" asked Dickie.

"Yes, as a matter of fact I did."

"Did you like it?"

"I was full of admiration. You knew I would be. Was there a breath of truth in it?"

"Naturally. At least, it's mostly true. She lives in a villa at Buyukdere. A very grand villa, thronging with servants. Far more like a palace, really. I only embroidered a very little. Not so you would notice."

"I expect the German Ambassador will notice."

"Do you think so, Addie? It's amazing what people will close their eyes to, you know."

"Not that sort of thing."

Dickie smiled in the direction of the waiter, a very beautiful young man with raven-black hair and flashing eyes. More raki. It's powerful stuff, it scrapes your throat as it goes down. Dickie is inured though, his throat is lined with steel.

"Is there any news of your great-aunt Lady Fanny?"

Dickie swallowed deeply, happily too.

"The very best, Addie. They say she's failing. Symptoms not unlike those of Mrs. Seawright. She has begun to muddle her words, the vision in her right eye is not what it should be . . . I've got a letter. It's from Miss Maria Branksome, her faithful companion. Shall I read it to you?"

He pronounced Maria as in <u>black</u> Maria. A lady who would otherwise have had smooth pink cheeks and smelled of lilies of the valley was at one stroke transformed into a black-moustachioed Tartar.

I swallowed a soupçon of my lemon tea. "No thank you. I couldn't bear it. One day I shall have to get old and decrepit myself, you see. Until then . . ."

Dickie will never grow old. He will always be exactly the same, even Lady Fanny's fortune will not change him.

"Are you finished with that tea of yours, Addie?"

"Yes. Almost. Now I have."

Dickie began sorting out money for the beautiful waiter, trying first one pocket and then the other.

"It's time we found a fly. We can't walk, I've drunk too much raki for that. And it's roasting hot. You did want to visit Lady Mary's villa, didn't you?"

Of course I did. I adore people's houses. There is nothing quite like them. Houses are full of secrets. Famous houses are especially intriguing but even the houses of your friends have their own smells, their own peculiar mysteries. Some people keep volumes of books beside their beds, others keep china barrels, full of biscuits. Some people wash their hands with scented soap, others employ treacle-coloured bars of Pears. These are all useful clues.

We walked around the outside of the house. I held Dickie's arm, thinking of the letters from Turkey. I wondered where she had sat in order to write them, whether she knew that she would be famous one day.

"Did she have a great many lovers?"

"Dozens, Addie. How can you doubt it?" Dickie's eyes were wicked and bright.

The village of Belgrad is built entirely of wood, surrounded by black walls. Tall cypress trees grow all around. Nowadays, Lady Mary would have required something grander, a palace by the Bosphorus like the German Ambassador's mistress, perhaps. La vie simple is quite out of fashion.

Later in the afternoon, we stopped at another café where a scented golden rose wandered along an ancient tumbled wall. Dickie drank more raki, I drank more tea. I told him about Rupert's visit to the Grand Vizier. From high above us there came a murmur of thunder. Droplets of rain fell on our table.

"Poor old Rupert, I don't see much hope, do you? Not that I ever did, did you? I wonder how it will take him."

"Badly, I should think. I have just begun to see that he is not very resilient."

"There are quite a lot of things that Rupert is not. I wonder that it has taken you so long to realize."

"I did realize, you know. I hoped that he would change. I am afraid that that is what women always do hope for."

"Do they? I had wondered."

"I think so. Lots of them, at least."

"And I wonder how things will turn out for the Sultan and the Viziers. Whether the reformers, chaps like Murat Bey, will have their way. We shouldn't view things too much in isolation, you know. Just Rupert and his difficulties."

"No, of course we shouldn't."

"Rain at last," said Dickie. "I had forgotten how very much I enjoy the pleasure of falling rain."

"Me too."

"Once I saw you coming down the steps of the Fitzwilliam, the rain sparkling in your hair. When you were young you were exceedingly beautiful, Addie. You laughed all the time as well. Laughing makes all the difference. Not like now, you know."

I stirred the slice of lemon which lay at the bottom of my

glass of tea. What else was there to do, after all? Dickie was only doing his best to enjoy the drama of the situation, reminding me that I might not be quite as old as Lady Fanny, but that even so . . .

"Come along now, let's not drown. Let us find a romantic vehicle. A fiacre, perhaps. You might develop pneumonia. There's rain running down your cheeks."

"I do remember that day, meeting you on the steps. I had my sketchbook with me, my charcoals too."

"Of course you remember. You have a perfect memory, Addie."

"That was when the world seemed full of nothing but statues and pictures, all sorts of things to walk out in the rain *for*, you see."

"And it still is, Addie. It still is."

*

Sam's reply came by return of post. No fond return of love, no kisses at the bottom, just this: "Look him up in the D.S.B. Thought even you would have heard of Walter Ramage."

No, of course not. I even had to think for a moment before I knew what the D.S.B. was. Then I got it. *Dictionary of Scientific Biography.*

Is Walter in the *Dictionary of Scientific Biography*?

*

Sunday.

Madame Chrissavelonis has arrived in a flurry of trunks and shiny hat boxes. The little girls are still tear-stained from their parting with their grandmama. Georges has remained behind in Smyrna. Perhaps he has taken ill, but no-one has said so. It is apparently considered quite in order for Madame C. to travel without him. Flora McPhee is grim-faced as ever, still swathed in black. She nodded to me in the salon this morning, cool as Scotch mist. Had I regaled myself with the celebrated antiquities of Stamboul? Yes, I had, I assured her. Mr. Nicolopulo was a guide sans pareil. And the little girls would especially enjoy the costumes at the Museum of Antiquities.

Mr. Nicolopulo, well.

It seems that he considers me to be a rapacious woman and cannot trust himself to drink tea with me.

He has sent me his manuscript, accompanied by this stiff little note:

My Dear Mrs. Renishaw,

I am to travel to Smyrna on the very first steamship that I can find. I enclose my address so that you may return my manuscript to me at your convenience, kind lady. There is illness in my little family. My second daughter has measles. My wife – a lady of uncertain temperament – is distraught. There is also another American party to be guided to the plains of Troy. I treasure your good opinion, Mrs. Renishaw, but as you see, I cannot drink tea with you. How does Miss Nettie go on? And the chère Madame? Pray do not think that I have forgotten our excursion to the garden of the seraglio.

He remains my obedient servant, he says.

I am determined that such a fate will not befall Maude Arabella, my unassailable heroine. Certainly not. Men will not suppose *her* to be rapacious, only alluring. My sole comfort is that Madame Nicolopulo has turned out to be a lady of uncertain temperament. That is not what I had supposed at all. A wife of uncertain temperament is a very grave obstacle to a man of ambition, as everybody agrees.

*

All day yesterday, I sat at my kitchen table with a green Venus pencil gripped tightly between my fingers. Would it help if I bought myself a word processor? No, of course not. By half-past three I have to put the light on, it's growing dark so early. In the garden of the house beneath my kitchen window there are bushes of brown and dripping hydrangea and ivy flowers in the shiny wet holly hedge.

In 1908, Walter won a Nobel prize for his investigations into the nature of matter. He died not long afterwards, in 1915. Just the same, I still know nothing at all about the remainder of his life. What happened to him between 1894 and 1915? If I don't discover more, Walter will never be anything but a straw-hatted gentleman, who once munched veal pie at Fenner's in the company of my great-grandmother, just as when I began to read these little notebooks Professor Mackintosh, my own great-great-grandfather, was nothing but a bearded gentleman in a daguerrotype, the possessor of a pair of embroidered slippers. What unfathomable mysteries they have both turned out to be . . .

And what am I to do about my soi-disant father, Felix? Do I really need to see him? After all, I have been managing without him since I was five years old. Perhaps I should write to Colonel Hevingham and find out the address of his old friend. I expect that the old friend might know where to find Felix. That would do no harm. I might propose a meeting, somewhere that is agreeable, somewhere I don't visit very often. Kew Gardens perhaps or the Sir John Soanes Museum, they would do. Better still, on reflection, there's a great deal to be said for the little bar at the Waldorf, the one on the edge of the Palm Court. Definitely somewhere with lashings of alcohol, I think.

*

In the afternoon I took Mr. N.'s manuscript to the rose garden. I have not described the rose garden but it lies beside the tennis court, within sound of the Bosphorus. Tennis balls ricocheted from the stiff and unrelenting net. A pair of German sisters, Luise and Theodora, pursued a sturdy game. They are visiting their distinguished brother, a blue-eyed diplomat with a faint violet line running down his cheek, a duelling scar acquired at the University of Göttingen. From time to time he can be observed to touch his scar, as though he were rather proud of it. Luise and Theodora dote on their brother but he hardly notices their presence. He is always busy waiting attendance upon the dubious Ambassador.

As I was setting out for the rose garden Rupert said, "Glad that Nicolopulo fellow's not trailing about anymore. I know you were fond of him, Addie, but anyone could tell that he was an oily stinker."

"Could they?"

"Naturally they could."

"Oilier than Doctor Banti, do you think?"

"Oh yes. No doubt about it. The doctor may be a rascally fake but he's not a stinker, is he?"

"Perhaps you are right. I am not quite certain. Isn't it time that we arranged to leave? What do you think, Rupert? Shall we go by way of Malta to Liverpool?"

An uncertain shadow swept across Rupert's face. He turned a little pale. I had discomfited him. He thrust his hands into his pockets like a boy; he blinked his pale eyelashes. Is he still hoping for a reprieve, a return of the Renishaw and Vignier investment, a lucrative piece of business? No, nothing like that. Something quite otherwise, I think.

"Not just yet," he said. "There are one or two things that I would like to attend to first."

And I expect there are.

In the rose garden I began to sniff an odd scent, the scent of powerful Turkish cigars. It was a smell which I associated with my journey through the Mediterranean, with silent Nettie, Stromboli and the saloon of the little ship *Tigre*. Were the German girls smoking forbidden cigars? No, of course they were not. Then who was?

*

PART FOUR

Therapia

T HE END OF the third leatherbound notebook. Adelina was correct in suspecting that it would not be amply capacious. (Amply capacious, there's an Adelina expression for you.)

I had hoped that the parts of her notebook would fall in perfect proportion – a three-volume account of her journey to Constantinople, but life and books are not the same, as everyone agrees. From now on there's nothing but a series of hastily scribbled pages attached by rusty dressmaker's pins. It's not always simple to decipher the chronology but I have done as best I can. I'm well acquainted with the notion that in life there are only events, never causes or effects, but in my opinion that's all it is, a notion – not in the least a useful one either.

In the meanwhile, there is news from the outer world. I shall write it down as quickly as possible so that I can return to my kitchen table (I'm on Chapter Three, getting along very nicely).

In the first place, Reginald is growing thinner and thinner. Almost every day now he travels to and from the vet's in his grand picnic hamper. He goes silently, rarely wailing or scuffling as he makes his journey up and down in the lift.

In the second place, there is news from Crick, Frick. It appears that the firm is about to be sold to a distinguished international consultancy. There is no chance of a buy-out succeeding at present. Management buy-outs no longer being the à la mode thing that they once were, it has turned out impossible for Marcus to raise the cash. The bank which was once so very kind and accommodating has now grown surly and unhelpful.

In any case, it appears that my work is going along far more smoothly than Adelina's.

*

Tuesday August 29th.

Yesterday I did nothing at all, only took to my chamber and read Lady Mary's letters, sulking. Now that Maude Arabella has fallen into the hands of Sir Piers Vicary, alias Sir Peter, I do not know quite what is to become of her. Naturally, it is my intention that Sir Piers will save Maude from the wicked Rumelian count – her greedy stepfather – that he will marry her, sweep her away to his estate in Lincolnshire and live happily ever afterwards. Just the same, I do not know quite how to catapult Sir Piers from villainy to heroism at a moment's notice. I am still awaiting inspiration.

This morning though, I exchanged words with Madame Chrissavelonis.

Madame was very pleased to see me. Her hair glittered with diamond clips. She was wearing Turkish dress, a jewelled girdle and many bracelets.

"And how are you, Madame? Are you well? I do hope so."

"I made a great many pictures during my days at Smyrna. One or two are rather good, I think. Apart from that . . ."

I remembered how we had stood on deck in the harbour of Smyrna, each making our own impression of the romantic landscape.

"And Monsieur Georges, how is he?"

Poor Monsieur, who so loves wine and delicacies of every sort. Does he know what is about to happen?

"I am afraid that he is the sort of man who requires devoted attention from his female relations. He is very happy in the company of his mother and sisters."

Yes, I expect he is. I have known others like him.

"Murat Bey was on board the steamer with me. There was a fierce storm in the night. We met in the salon. Everyone else was locked in their cabins. You could hear them groaning."

I enquired after the two little girls, Alice and Dora.

"You would have thought that they were the only little girls ever born. Everyone in Smyrna thought highly of them. They are considered to possess fine manners and delicate musical apprehension. Everyone is agreed that they will become famous beauties. Still, they do not have Greek names. That is considered a point against them. In Smyrna, my husband's relations call me The English woman and say that I am cold and hard-hearted. They are very afraid that the girls will grow up to be like me."

Is she hard-hearted and cold? No, not for a moment. It would be a calumny even to suppose it. Apart from her astonishing beauty, vitality and warmth are Madame's finest qualities.

"Not cold-hearted. Indifferent, I think. That is what we are. But you need not worry. You are Greek, and the Greeks are celebrated for their warmth and wisdom and beauty."

This studied praise delighted Madame. She adjusted one of her diamond clips, thinking what she might say next.

"Tell me, do you play tennis?"

But she knows as well as I do that I do not.

"No."

"Then may I ask something of you?"

"Yes, of course."

"You did speak of the girls, didn't you?"

"Mmm, I did."

"I was thinking. Perhaps a little excursion. Naturally, Flora would accompany you. Tomorrow afternoon, would that be agreeable? To Scutari? You might tell Alice and Dora the story of Florence Nightingale. I am playing in a tournament, you see."

Yes, why not? I have not visited Scutari, after all. You can still see the Haidar Pasha Military Hospital and even the British cemetery. I would like to inspect the little room where Florence wrote all those business-like letters to Sidney Herbert. And I shall enjoy telling the girls the story of *The Lady With The Lamp*. It is an exemplary story, quite the story of thing which ought to be told to little girls.

"It would be an enormous pleasure, Madame."

Really. A tournament indeed.

*

Another lunch with Julia. Far more abstemious this time, no moules or Calvados. I find that office lunches are one thing which I do not miss. I took my chapters with me. I had written them on green unlined W.H. Smith's notebooks. I know that anyone possessing the least speck of virtue would write on brown and porridgey recycled paper but I'm exceedingly fond of smooth and creamy pages.

Julia said, "I'm abandoning Philippe. I've explained to the children. They understand perfectly."

"Good."

What a lot children are required to understand nowadays. And was Philippe her second husband? It was not the moment to enquire. Julia's men are all alike, handsome and ill-tempered. It's always possible that I've forgotten someone, you never know. But no, how horrid I am becoming. Of course Philippe is her second husband. What am I thinking of?

"You can grow tired of a person. In the end you begin to know them far too well, so that there's nothing left to discover. In the beginning Philippe pretended not to mind whenever I put Marmite into his onion soup. He would smile gently, as if I couldn't help being a barbarian. Then he gave up all pretence and began to get livid at the very sniff of it. Only English people like Marmite, have you noticed?"

"Australians too, I think. Or something very like it."

"Did Sam like Marmite?"

"No."

"Even the arguments become boring, not to mention the . . ."

"I have heard that said."

"There it is. Naturally, I've got someone else lined up."

Do I perhaps envy Julia? No. Envy is melting away as I grow older. Jealousy though is always with me, I am afraid.

"Anyone I know?"

Julia's smile radiated. "No, Penelope. No-one you know. And don't you think you'd better give me those chapters that you've written? You have brought them with you, haven't you? You do want me to let you know if they're rubbish, don't you? A.S.A.P.?"

I thought for a moment. A.S.A.P. – as soon as possible. I had discovered one or two alarmingly grey hairs that morning. They were affecting my judgement, I'm ashamed to say. They made me wonder whether I really wanted Julia's advice about my biography after all, whether I didn't in fact prefer to carry on with my own life in my own way from now on.

Naturally, Julia does not believe in grey hair; she will never allow herself any. Grey hair will not affect her opinions.

"Not yet," I said. "Anyway, they're still handwritten. In little notebooks, with a Venus pencil. You wouldn't approve."

"Better hurry up," said Julia. "I've had a very nice offer from a media consultancy group, you know. I shall be losing some of my useful contacts."

"Coffee?"

"Coffee's bad for you, Penelope. I should have thought you knew that."

When it arrived, Julia drank her coffee neatly and reflectively. As I am addicted to caffeine, I drank mine greedily, swilled it down and sent for more.

"What was her essential quality, do you suppose?" enquired Julia.

"Whose?"

"Adelina's, silly."

"Energy."

"What, when she spent all those years lying on a sofa, doing nothing but reading books from Mudie's?"

"Mmm, I think so. It's the conclusion I've come to. And she was reading the right books, remember."

"I believe in keeping busy," said Julia firmly. "I never have a spare moment, I'm always booked up."

Luckily, I still had a drop of red wine left.

"All famous people have dormant stretches, Julia. They prepare in silence. There are a great many precedents."

"But she wasn't famous."

"She was once. And she will be again when I'm finished with her."

"Would that please her, do you think?"

"I am afraid that it would. Quite a lot too."

"And have you discovered who your great-grandpapa was?"

"I've known from the very beginning."

"Really?"

"I read the ending first."

Julia's eyes widened, a characteristic gesture. She tapped her spoon against her glass.

"I'd forgotten that you did that."

"Mmm, yes. Still do."

"Was it a surprise?"

"Not exactly. It was the obvious suspect all along, just like Agatha Christie. The bit in the middle was a red herring."

Julia is very acute. That is the secret of her success. You cannot hide a weakness from her. She hones in upon it immediately. Her nicely plucked eyebrows went flying upwards.

"Just like Agatha Christie. How very suspicious. You must sort it out, you know. If you have doubts. You can't just leave it hanging."

"I suppose not. I'll have to see what I can do."

There followed a moment of silence. I found a credit card, Julia found crisp folded notes, straight from a machine.

"Do you really think that it was energy?" asked Julia eventually. "And if it was, where did all that energy come from?"

Perhaps she was thinking of her own booked-up life, she sounded very pensive.

"I'm not completely sure, I've got an idea though."

"Go on then."

"It's only a notion, you see. That's all."

"Do get on with it. I've got a meeting."

"It comes of knowing that you are in the right, I'm afraid. Being absolutely, positively certain of it. Whether you are or not. It's doubt that saps your energy. Depression. Accidie."

Julia waved her hands in the air. She has always manicured her hands, painted her toenails, got up early in order to curl her hair.

"But what about Florence? What about Elizabeth Barrett Browning? Even Edith Cavell . . ."

"They got over it," I said tartly. "They had strength of conviction. They were brave. They were <u>not like us</u>."

"I've sometimes thought that they were mad," stated Julia. "Don't you think they were?"

I shook my head. "No, definitely not. No worse than the rest of us."

"Oh well." Julia was consulting her *Financial Times* engagement diary, seeing whether she had forgotten any of the afternoon's appointments.

"Shall we go?"

"I think so, don't you?"

But they weren't mad. At least, I don't suppose so. They didn't go into analysis with expensive charlatan doctors, or spend their time in endless, boring meetings, that much is certain.

"See you," said Julia.

"I do hope so," I replied.

*

Written at the rosewood table in my bed chamber, before dawn on Thursday.

When we had returned from the excursion to Scutari, Flora waved her black bombazined arms, sweeping the two little girls away.

"You two, in the bath. This instant. We cannot have your Mama seeing you in this state. What a disgrace!"

"Alice smells," said Dora, who is small and plump and dark. She is the very image of Monsieur Georges, her father, and is most unlikely ever to become a famous beauty. Nevertheless, she will grow up to be intelligent and good, qualities which are not to be sneezed at.

"Alice has a delicate stomach," said Flora, chilly with self-righteousness.

"Poor Alice. It was all my fault. Nothing to do with her."

"You should not have allowed sherbet and ice cream together, if you don't mind my saying so. That was a grave mistake. Anyone can see that you are not used to children, Madam."

"No. You are quite right."

"Come along, girls. Say thank you."

They disappeared, Flora entirely gratified. I found Rupert and Madame drinking together in the garden. They sat at a white ironwork table. Madame appeared serene and calm, her hair smelled newly washed. Rupert presented a contrast. He was rather pink, a drop of sweat lingering on his upper lip. He was missing a shirt stud too, I could not help noticing.

"Tea, my dear?"

As I no longer believe whole-heartedly in the restorative powers of tea, I replied that I would rather drink a glass of champagne, pink champagne if that were possible. I am afraid that this alarmed Rupert. He thought it a sign of gloomy spirits. He got out his pocket watch, tapped it, sighed. I could tell that it was preposterously early, far too early for anything but a soothing cup of tea in Rupert's opinion. So much in life does turn out to depend upon timing. Nevertheless.

"Champagne, Rupert," commanded Madame, with all the confidence of a lady who is something more than simply a *shipboard acquaintance*.

Rupert was looking dazed, perhaps even a little glum. I could not help but notice that the German girls at the next table were studying us with close attention. Luise sat beneath a parasol, Theodora was composing a letter. Just the same, there was no disguising their curiosity.

"I am afraid that Alice was sick on the steamer," I announced. "It was all my fault. Flora McPhee said so."

Madame gave the sort of shrug which mothers generally do give when they are informed that their children have vomited. You detect a note of gratitude that they were not present.

"I expect they had a glorious time. Children are generally sick whenever things are especially exciting. I hope you told them all about Florence."

I said that I had, in great detail too. I did not add that Scutari, being in the Asian part of the city, was in itself a thoroughly educational place to visit and quite in contrast to the embassies of Therapia and Buyukdere.

"You are looking pale," said Madame kindly. "You should take my shawl. The wine will chill you."

<u>They</u> were not drinking tea but Turkish coffee, solid, black and sweet. The garden of the Summer Palace Hotel was full of birds, Luise and Theodora were deciding whether or not to eat another plate of cakes. Madame's shawl was neither warm nor heavy but simply a long whisper of Brussels lace. It smelled disagreeably of Madame's scent and Rupert's brilliantine hair oil, a horrid mélange.

When my pink champagne arrived, I drank it thirstily.

"Another glass, I suppose?" grumbled Rupert.

"Yes, please."

There is a great deal to be said for champagne of any variety, as most people agree. It is not to be compared with the ginger wine of my girlhood. By now Luise and Theodora had decided against another instalment of cakes. They were preparing to go, reluctantly, I could tell.

"I do hope that you will dine with me this evening," said Madame. "I hate sitting at a table by myself. We must have a special fish. The Bosphorus is renowned for its fish, you know."

Let them carry on without <u>me</u>, I thought. It is not as though they require a chaperone.

"And afterwards there will be dancing," sighed Madame contentedly.

As we were getting up, I could not help noticing certain

features of Madame's appearance – her cherry-coloured dorothy bag, her scent, her gloves and narrow waist. When I thought that Rupert was making love to Miss Watson the typewriter, I spent my days striding up and down the house like an angry cat, forever muttering: "Why does he want <u>her</u>? What is so tempting about <u>her</u>?"

With Madame C., there is no need to pose such questions. She is beautiful and well-behaved, amiable too, and even her own husband is content to surrender to her pleasures. No wonder other men fall in with equanimity.

"And what about your tournament?" I could not help asking, failing perhaps to stifle a certain acid note.

They turned to one another, without words for a moment. I believe that it was in this instant that Rupert noticed his missing stud. A vein began to beat in his neck. He ran his fingertips through his hair.

Madame spoke first; she had perhaps not noticed Rupert's déshabille.

"Miss Nettie could not play. The tournament was abandoned. We will carry on tomorrow instead. Perhaps you might take her place? They say that Mrs. Seawright is dying, you know."

*

But how can Mrs. Seawright be dying? It's impossible. There must be some misunderstanding. I have grown fond of Mrs. Seawright, her portmanteau full of books and her generosity with the brandy bottle.

Yesterday I received a note from my.father, Felix. It appears that Colonel Hevingham's old friend received my letter and sent it to him directly. We are to meet the day after tomorrow, at six o'clock in the bar at the Waldorf. I don't know what to wear. I don't want to appear to have dressed up especially. On the other hand, I don't want to be too dishevelled and unkempt. I am not an entirely disreputable person, after all. Perhaps I should have my hair cut. I might get out one of my navy blue suits, I haven't worn one for quite a long time now. What would Camilla wear? What would Victoria wear? What would Julia wear? What am I going to wear?

*

Thursday. 11 a.m.

This morning Madame C. came to present me with evidence of Rupert's dalliance, a pearl stud wrapped in thin, scented, rustling paper – stuffing from the toes of one of her narrow Italian shoes.

As I was writing at my rosewood table in the middle of the night, it had come to me that I was not in the least jealous, that I did not long to keep Rupert forever to myself but that I was suffering from a fault even more shameful still. I was envious. I did not want Rupert to love Madame because I did not want him to know pleasure with her. As for Madame . . .

When she arrived at my door I was lying in my deep porcelain bathtub, contemplating the black and white tiles – deep, steamy, scalding baths being one of the very best remedies for self-pity that I have ever discovered.

I threw on a silky wrapper. The ends of my wet hair streamed upon my shoulders. I thought, "It is Mrs. Seawright."

But instead, it was Madame, wearing a walking costume of dove-grey. Her in-laws in Smyrna would not have been surprised to see her in this business-like garb, they would have expected it.

She was not in the least downcast. Her wonderful dark eyes – but no, there's been far too much of that sort of thing in these pages, glimmering pools of jet and so on. I must guard expressions of that sort for Maude Arabella and company, and not allow melodrama to seep into the pages of my sensible diary.

The significant detail was this – Madame C. was in perfect command of herself. She neither stammered nor trembled. I detected no note of pity in her appearance, only a certain briskness.

"Perhaps you recognize this? It is a pearl stud. Do you see?"

Of course I did. I clutched my silky wrapper, glad that she had not sent Flora with the stud. Flora thinks harshly enough of me as it is without knowing that I am a betrayed wife. On the other hand though, what must Flora suppose about Madame, her mistress?

In an astonishingly casual way, Madame began to tell me that she was departing very soon, travelling by the fabled Orient Express, visiting her cousin in Sofia and her brother in Vienna – her relations being so usefully scattered about the world. I thought of hot Balkan plains, black jagged mountain peaks and fierce politics. What a miraculous escape. Lucky Madame. Envy struck at me once again. Perhaps in my next life I should _travel_ more?

"But what am I supposed to do with this?"

I am afraid that I sounded rather plaintive, not in the least grateful, as I should have been.

Madame glanced at me rather sharply.

"Take it," she said loftily. "Do whatever you would like. But you cannot pretend that it didn't happen."

No, that is exactly what I do not relish about the situation.

"An antidote to those mountains of fat books you so delight in. This is true, books are not."

I spent rather a long time looking down at the stud, turning it over, considering the life-line of my right hand.

"Thank you."

"No need to thank me," said Madame briskly. "On the contrary."

"Do you always do whatever you would like, turning the tables and that sort of thing?"

"I have explained to you, Adelina. Life does not last very long. It's a woman's duty to be happy. It's far kinder to her husband. In marriage there must always be a certain measure of diversion. And you should return my shawl to me before I go. You do not enjoy the smell of it."

I fetched the shawl, handed it to her. We both sniffed her scent, Rupert's hair oil too. I smiled.

"Goodbye. Please give my love to Alice and Dora."

I could not help but notice that, dearly as I would like to avoid the expression, Madame's eyes were indeed glimmering – Madame being one of those lucky people who are forever amused by the curious eventualities of her life.

"Now that we are friends, you must pronounce my name, and not call me Madame all the time, as though I were nothing but an old dragon of your acquaintance. It is a pretty name, Mariora. You must use it."

But I already have, I already have.

*

In the end, I allowed myself to be influenced by Madame C. and bought a dove-grey suit. It is a French suit, simple and charming. I purchased finely sculpted boots. I adore boots. I looked out one of Adelina's silver belt buckles and folded my hair into a Charlotte Brontë chignon. The past is not simply our inheritance; it is also a dressing-up box, I am afraid.

"What will you drink, Penelope?"

"Gin and tonic, please."

"I thought that nowadays young people drank nothing but white wine."

"Perhaps they do. But I'm no longer young, you see. I am thirty-eight years old. And I would definitely like gin and tonic."

"Then you shall have it."

"Thank you."

"You are wondering what you should call me, I expect."

"I think that perhaps 'Felix' would be best, don't you?"

"You would hardly want to call me 'Father'."

"No, quite."

"I haven't been here since 1947, you know. I come to London very seldom. The first night of our honeymoon was spent at this place. Your grandmother, a lady who was renowned for her generosity, footed the bill. The next day we travelled to Paris. The weather was most unhelpful, our ferry couldn't dock immediately. There were chairs and tables flying about. Sea-sickness is so very disagreeable. Not the recommended way to begin your honeymoon, I'm afraid. It has often crossed my mind that perhaps . . ."

"And is it true that my mother wore long johns underneath her wedding dress?"

My father smiled, taking a long swig of his drink.

"Perfectly. You've no idea how cold it was. Never been so frozen since. I have taken pains not to be."

I must say that I found this absorbing news. Paris, honeymoons, the celebrated winter of 1947. I was longing to get out my notebook. My memory isn't as sharp as it once was, I can't be relied on to retain the salient points. I munched my cheese straws, sipped my own drink — thought ungratefully that however good my gin was, it would have been far better made with lime rather than lemon. I wondered whether they too had enjoyed tempting dinners at Prunier's, starlit perambulations in the Champs de Mars.

"Perhaps you would like to know about my mother?" I enquired tartly. "What happened to her, that sort of thing?"

"The other Penelope. Yes indeed, do tell me about her. Naturally. Is she flourishing?"

I took another sip, waited a moment.

"She's dead, as a matter of fact."

"Ah! Peacefully, I do hope."

"No, not very."

In the end they put her on a morphine drip. Julia would have been relieved to learn that by the time of her death my mother was very thin indeed, not a speck of fat to be found on her bones.

He didn't say that he was sorry; he didn't say anything at all. He made himself useful, he got us both another drink. I like the bar at the Waldorf. It's a fine place for cold drinks and bad news. I resolved to visit it far more often, though if I'm giving up my job at Crick, Frick, it'll be harder to afford in the future.

"In your letter you said that you were writing a book about your great-grandmother."

"Mmm, yes. But I don't think that I shall ever know her."

"No?"

"Dead people are even more unfathomable than live ones. For a long while I thought that it was the other way around."

"Did you, indeed?"

"I'm afraid so. And I am afraid of making her up as well. With live people, you see, the evidence keeps flooding in. With dead ones there comes a point when one has to suppose things."

I could tell that that thought interested him. It interested me too. We do so long to believe that our version of people's lives is the correct one, the truth.

My father began to speak.

"I was an admirer of hers, you know; Penelope took me to stay with her once. Christmas 1944, the time of the fighting around Bastogne. Our train was very late. Penelope was obliged to wash her hair in the w.c.. We sat on a crate of oranges belonging to some Canadian soldiers."

It was rather odd, the way he kept saying 'Penelope', but did not in the least mean me.

It occurred to me that my mother had overflowed with quick, revealing, untrammelled emotions. My father, on the other hand, was not in the least like that. He had, I thought, a proud, hard, prickly centre. I expect that they made one another very unhappy.

"Adelina thought that you were a coward. She told me so when I was a little girl."

My father laughed. It was a wry laugh. Would he have agreed that marriage requires diversion?

"Because I ran away from your mother?"

"Exactly."

"She advised us that second marriages were always best. 'Hurry up and get the first one over with as quickly as possible, my second husband was far nicer than my first', she said."

I sat up in my chair, gin and tonic spilling down the front of my extravagant grey suit, ice tinkling in the heavy glass.

"What? What did you say? What's this about two husbands?"

My father handed me a handkerchief of the starched, white, old-fashioned sort.

"Didn't you know?"

I must say he appeared delighted with himself.

"Of course not. Get on with it. Who on earth was he?"

"I don't know. Let me see . . . Perhaps . . ."

"Well, really. Didn't you meet him as well?"

"I would remember, I'm not entirely gaga. He was dead. Yes, that was it, he was absolutely dead. I encountered an old friend of your great-grandmother's, though. A very unreliable character, I should think. Well-known for cheating at cards, I heard."

"Dickie."

"That's it. Wait a moment. It's coming to me now."

"Oh good, I'm so glad."

I bit into a very salty peanut. On one side of us there was an American lady sipping a whisky and soda, sliding her feet out of her agonizing shoes while her husband perused his copy of the *A–Z*. On my other side there was a kindly Indian gentleman attired in his magnificent evening finery. I know that he was kindly because of his habit of looking about at everyone, glancing at them with absorption and concern.

"I've got it. Walter something."

Walter. Well, really. Walter.

How amazing. Walter.

And then I thought, how lovely, how nice. Really and truly. So she married Walter in the end. Why did no-one bother to tell me? Extraordinary.

"Extraordinary."

"I'm glad that I have been useful to you, after all."

"Quite. Me too."

"How thoroughly British you are, Penelope. All you say is Quite, Extraordinary and Exactly. You have no idea of conversation, have you? The British are so very proud of themselves. And for so little reason."

"English," I said absently. "I'm not British, I'm English. And it's all your fault, anyway. I can't think why you're grumbling about it."

Right then and there it occurred to me that Adelina was thoroughly English too. Never mind the fact that she fell for dark-haired foreign gentlemen, never mind the fact that she adored the hot, gritty station at Smyrna and the thronging cavernous bazaar at Constantinople. She was like Dickie's great-aunt Lady Fanny Addiscombe, like all those redoubtable ladies, Florence and the rest, thoroughly English. Once they had roused themselves to defy their own mutton-chop-whiskered, beef-eating papas the rest of the world posed no obstacles whatsoever, so great was their unerring sense of absolute superiority.

"Shall we have dinner?" my father enquired. "There's a fish restaurant I'm fond of, not far away."

"Why not?" I said. "You must tell me everything that you remember about Adelina. And about my aunts in Cracow as well. I especially want to know if any of them are like me. You won't mind if I bring out my notebook at the dinner table, will you?"

*

Saturday, August 30th. Written after lunch.

As I suspected, the aromatic scent of cigars belonged to Murat Bey.

It is so like the last act of a comic opera, everyone dashing on to the stage all at once. Why is Mr. Murat Bey not busy capturing bandits in the province of Smyrna?

"There is a quota," he laughed. "And I have met mine."

I came across him down by the quayside today, while I was out walking. The quay at Therapia is where famous people parade, diplomats and pashas, all manner of beautiful ladies. It is a sort of pump room at Bath; you may expect to encounter everyone there sooner or later. Do not suppose for a moment though, that I have forgotten that in Smyrna he did not even say goodbye to me. I was decidedly cool. I fixed my gaze on the sparkling blue waters and the progress of the many white-sailed caiques.

"Your quota for the month?" I enquired.

"For the year," he replied.

As it happened, Nettie was strolling with me. I had been telling her the story of Maude Arabella, Sir Piers Vicary and the wicked count. "It's not to be compared with Ouida. All the same, perhaps it will amuse you. It's just the thing to read while you are staying up all night with an invalid," I told her.

When he saw Nettie, one of Mr. Murat Bey's black eyebrows went whizzing upwards, as if to say, "There you are. What did I tell you? See how she flourishes."

Mr. Murat Bey has reminded me (as if I had forgotten) that once I promised to attend the ceremony of the Selamlik with him. It is arranged that we are to go together on Friday.

"Shall I see the Sultan?" I asked.

To which he replied that the Sultan did not enjoy being inspected by ladies, especially foreign ladies. Ladies and gentlemen, he explained, are not expected to look upon one another. That is the very height of indignity.

Only think. If Elizabeth Bennet had never actually <u>seen</u> Mr. Darcy. There would have been no novel at all. But Moslems of course do not believe in graven images, artless decoration, any more than the Puritans did.

"Just the same," he said. "If the circumstances are fortuitous . . ."

I do not think that <u>he</u> finds me rapacious. If he does, I suspect that perhaps he rather enjoys it.

*

The circumstances have not been fortuitous for Mrs. Munns or for poor Reginald, who died yesterday afternoon.

"They put him to sleep," said Mrs. Munns sadly. "I left him at the vet's. I haven't even got a garden to bury him in."

"Never mind. He won't know, I'm sure of that."

"No, I suppose not."

"I think that the nineteenth century was the best time for graves and memorials, don't you agree? For dogs as well as people. Have you ever visited the dogs' graves at Sandringham?"

"Of course," said Mrs. Munns.

"It's not as if they do much for people nowadays, is it?"

"I should say not. They'd put us in black plastic sacks if they could get away with it."

"Still, I don't know why animals can't live as long as we do. It seems such a lopsided arrangement."

"It's all arranged abominably, if you ask me. Men are supposed to be so resilient, but then we have no difficulty in outlasting them, do we?"

"No. We don't."

"They're not very durable, are they?"

"No, they're not."

"They drop like flies."

"They do, don't they?"

"I shan't remain here forever. Now that Reginald is dead, I shall go and live with my daughter in Scotland."

Mrs. Munns could not help sounding rather proud, as if it were not everyone who had a daughter in Scotland with whom they might go to live.

"The one in Ross and Cromarty?"

"Susanna. She hates cats, you know."

No, I didn't know. How hideous children can be. How unaccountable in their affections. How strange it is that in some ways they are the very images of their parents, in other ways quite foreign people altogether . . .

*

Sunday. 5.00 p.m.

By now, I have composed myself. I have completed my reading of Mr. N.'s guide book and have written a solemn letter to him, telling him of everything that I thought while reading his pages. His prose is very exact and therefore very dull. There is nothing to be compared with Mrs. Elliot's description of the pitiful stray dogs of Constantinople or the round and painted faces of the grandest

Ottoman ladies, not to mention the Vicomte's glowing and scented account of the harbour. Mr. N. leaves out no detail, thus defying Mademoiselle Aimée's instructions about the composition of a first-rate diary.

Just the same, there is something to be said for Mr. N.'s exertions. It is indubitably very useful to be told that money is not worth the same at Smyrna as at Stamboul. Pointers of this kind are sorely needed in life as well as journeys.

I wrote kind and gracious things, as was expected of me. It is perhaps the last time that I shall do exactly what is expected of me. I hoped that his daughters were lively as kittens. I confided that Miss Nettie was going on splendidly but that Mrs. S.'s condition gave cause for unrivalled alarm. And then, for good measure – and out of wickedness too – I wrote, "*I shall not say adieu, Monsieur, but only au revoir, for it is possible that we shall meet again in Smyrna in the course of my journey home.*"

But it is not possible. It is impossible. This is the absolute end of Mr. Demetri Nicolopulo. He has been a very grave disappointment to me. I shall discipline myself not to think of him ever again. I shall especially not think of his voice and the way in which it used to cause my spine to shiver. I shall not think of our journey in the train to Ephesus together, nor of Demetrius the Silversmith. There are a great <u>many</u> things which I shall never contemplate again.

In case it should come in handy, I enclose his description of the Sultan's palace at Yildiz:

The palace is beautifully situated on the heights above Cheragan, and has a large park surrounded by lofty walls. The views from the windows over the park and the Bosporous to the Asiatic Coast are very beautiful. The park is charmingly laid out, and contains several picturesque kiosks and sheets of ornamental water.

*

But should I believe in Mr. Nicolopulo?

I didn't want to discuss the matter with Julia, she would not have been sympathetic. Just the same, I've got to make up my mind, take a view, decide what I'm going to think.

But what am I going to think? That's the question. I've been keeping this doubt to myself for a very long time now. What shall I do about it?

There's no doubt that Adelina made things up. She made up Maude Arabella and, as it turns out, Rupert was of the opinion that she had made him up as well. Just the same, there is no doubt that people who never make anything up generally don't get fat biographies written about them. Famous people are very careful to make themselves up. They burn their letters and tell particular stories to their grandchildren. There is a point of improbability, a mystery, in everyone's life.

There is no copy of Mr. N.'s book to be found in any of the libraries which I frequent. No-one has written his biography. He is not mentioned in the letters of other travellers to Turkey.

I shall have to begin a round of the second-hand bookshops, launch inquiries, see what I can find.

*

Midnight, Sunday.

Tomorrow afternoon I am to be allowed to pay a visit to Mrs. Seawright. Nettie says that she has been packaging her books for me, wrapping them in brown paper and ribbon so that I may take them home to my house in good order. She adds that I will find her mama's condition greatly changed, and for the worse at that. She is suffering harsh pain, Nettie says, and her attention has begun to wander from time to time.

I shall not tell her that I have almost decided never to return to my house and that in future I shall not have nearly so much room for books.

*

Yesterday I had a telephone call from Marcus. Is it very unkind to suppose that people like Marcus Monckton-Smith are a good deal easier to comprehend than Madame C. or Adelina? In any case, whoever it was who said, "Tout comprendre, c'est tout pardonner" was fatally wrong. Our conversation went something like this:

"I wanted you to be the first to know, Penelope. Camilla and I are reconciled."

"I'm so glad, Marcus. I'm sure it's the best thing for both of you."

"So am I. How nice of you to say so. We are moving to Suffolk. I shall catch the train in Ipswich every morning. Everyone tells me that the line into Liverpool Street is definitely not to be recommended. Still. No more dilapidated cottages though. We are going to build a house."

Mr. Blandings Builds His Dream House, Cary Grant and Myrna Loy, of course. One of my favourites.

"Lovely. Lucky you."

"And I wanted to thank you."

"Whatever for?"

"For soothing poor Camilla the other day. She was in rather a state, poor old thing. You took care of her. Victoria told me all about it, you know."

"Mmm, ah, Victoria, yes. Actually, Marcus, she seemed all right to me."

"Victoria?"

"No, Camilla."

"Do you think so?"

"Yes, I do. Definitely."

"How very odd." Marcus sounded most discomfited.

"Perhaps I got the wrong end of the stick."

"I rather think you must have done, Penny. If you don't mind my saying so."

I pictured Marcus running a hand across the top of his head, ironing flat his curly hair. I pictured his face, red and bumpy with exasperation, as it always is when you do not see things quite as he does.

"I'm so sorry."

Marcus harrumphed.

"Poor old Cam was pretty cut up, you know."

"I didn't mean to suggest . . ."

"You've got an unkind streak, Penelope. I'm a pretty observant chap. I notice these things."

"All's well that ends well, Marcus."

"Anyway, I just wanted to thank you. And I'm leaving Crick, Frick by the way. Can't say more just at present. Must be discreet. A definite leg up though."

"Splendid news. And you were kind to me too once, if you remember."

"Can't say I do, Penny. Can't say I do. So long. We'll invite you for a weekend in the country one day."

"Goodbye, Marcus."

"Or perhaps we should lunch together? What a good idea. Shall we say Tuesday? Monday's my luncheon club, Thursday I'm in Frankfurt. Tuesday it is, I'll pencil you in."

"No, thank you. Please don't. The thing is I –"

"I could just about manage Friday. It'll have to be somewhere nearby though. We shan't have long. What a nuisance you are, Penelope. I'm frightfully busy. Still, make it Friday."

I put the telephone down. There was no alternative. That's the one really good thing about the parlous state of our telephone service. It's so easy to say "Heavens, no, did you really ring me eight times? How odd. I was in all evening, you know. Honestly, they are hopeless. And to think that they don't even bother to itemize the bills. What a swindle."

And then, of course, I unplugged my phone.

*

Tuesday, September now.

Mrs. Seawright is dead. The news came to me this morning with my glass of lemon tea. I shall now write an account of my last visit to her.

When I entered, Nettie was standing at her mother's bedside, wafting the sandalwood fan to and fro. The portmanteau full of books and the bottle of brandy were nearby.

I am afraid that I took one of Mrs. S.'s cigarettes, breathing in the smoke very deeply.

Nettie and her mother appeared quite composed. Mrs. Seawright was not attired in her green kimono, but in a white nightdress of starched cotton and simple crocheted lace. Nettie too was wearing one of the white dresses which she had worn upon the steamer, in the days when she was pretending to love Murat Bey. It gave her the air of someone very calm and pure and young – all the things she is, in fact.

At first observation, you might have supposed Mrs. Seawright's condition to have grown better, her face was exceedingly rubicund, her eyes very bright. Upon closer inspection though, it was plain that her face was dark with blood and swollen. Her left arm worked very clumsily and her eyes did not see quite as they should have done. They were filmy as a sick cat's. She was sitting upright, a lap desk resting upon her bed covers.

"I am composing my will," said Mrs. Seawright. "I have summond Mr. Frank Calvert, the American Consul, to witness it for me, and Doctor Faulkner, my American doctor."

"Not Doctor Banti?"

"Doctor Banti's strength lies in the giving of comforts rather than the giving of cures. If you wanted to murder your husband then the dottore would be your man. Otherwise . . ."

But of course, Mrs. Seawright was beyond cure, as no-one doubted. Nettie brought an embroidered chair and I sat at the bedside.

Mrs. Seawright held a swollen finger in the air. A beat or two of silence. Then she began to speak.

It has been decided that Nettie is to be allowed to marry whomever she pleases. Mrs. Seawright has already written to Mr. Grimwade, Nettie's trustee, telling him so. She will inherit her fortune outright and can do whatever she likes with it.

"Nettie shall live in idle luxury for the rest of her days. She will give first-rate balls and serve on committees. For that sort of thing you require a good deal of money. I would not want her to go penniless among the aristocracy. At least it cannot be said that this young man of hers is marrying her for her money."

"No, of course not. You must not trouble about Nettie. She is a very strong-minded girl."

Nettie only smiled at this, bringing me a little tot of brandy as she did so.

"In my opinion all girls are strong-minded. The question is, are they *right-minded*?"

We sipped our brandy while I remembered that Mrs. Seawright had never felt a breath of sympathy for romance and could not be expected to begin now.

"And as for you, my dear . . ."

"I have brought you some of my drawings of Stamboul, Mrs. Seawright. I hoped they would amuse you. There's one of the garden at the Seraglio, another of Lady Mary Wortley Montague's villa, where Dickie Ricardo took me."

"Nettie tells me that you are writing a story."

"Not the sort that you would approve of, dear Mrs. Seawright. It is a romantic fantasy."

It occurred to me to enquire of Mrs. Seawright whether she considered that life was more important than books. I did not add that this was Dickie's opinion, Madame C.'s, Rupert's too, if it came to that.

"Of course it is," exclaimed Nettie. "What a ridiculous question. Really, Mrs. Renishaw."

But Mrs. Seawright did not answer immediately. She drank a little brandy – which was only making her face all the ruddier – and I could tell that she was finding her glass exceedingly heavy. In the end she told me that she had never been able to do without either one, but that if the life were any good, or the books any good, then they would stand together, perfectly undivided.

This seemed to me to be such a very <u>balanced</u> opinion that there was really very little left to say on the subject. Without life there would be no books, and the other way round too, of course.

Just the same, we do expect dying people to give us lots of answers.

"And what about love?" I enquired.

But at the mention of love, Mrs. Seawright only sighed, indicating that Nettie should pour her a drop more brandy. Nettie herself was prancing about, rosy and assured, as people do when they are in the thick of love.

When the brandy had arrived, Mrs. Seawright swirled it in her glass.

"I am afraid that I have nothing very comforting to say on the subject of love. Except that it is possible to do without it, if you must. There are other things, brandy and books, for example. Property too, I am sorry to say."

And at the mention of the word 'property', Mrs. Seawright glanced at me sternly, as if to remind me that I had none.

"Do look at my pictures." I said, feeling a desperate need to interrupt. "And then I shall read you the ending of my story. Nettie likes it, don't you, Nettie?"

"I think so," said Nettie politely. "You'd better listen to what Mama has to say."

"Property," said Mrs. Seawright once again.

"Do listen," said Nettie.

"Fold your hands," commanded Mrs. Seawright. "Sit nicely. I haven't got all the time in the world."

"I want you to know that it was all my idea," said Nettie. "In case there is any misunderstanding."

"Quiet, Nettie."

Once upon a time such a peremptory command would have crumpled Nettie's spirits, now though, she bore it cheerfully.

Mrs. Seawright proceeded to light one of her thin black cigarettes. The match smelled sulphurous. The blue smoke whirled. At first her voice was very gravelly and deep, her words falling like lumps of inert matter.

"When I learned about the regrettable shortcomings of your learned papa, the gentleman who is so misguided as to favour ginger wine . . . Well, my dear . . ."

"Don't stop now, Mama. Carry on."

"Don't interrupt me, Nettie."

"No, no, of course I shan't."

"I decided that I would make a certain provision for you too, my dear. In my will. That is to say . . . In any case, it is all settled. I have arranged it with Mr. Grimwade."

Mrs. Seawright, like an old dragon, puffed out a cloud of smoke. I, for my part, was beginning to grow oddly accustomed to the notion that my dear Papa might be questioned, perhaps even held in deprecation.

"I have always been of the opinion that a man who is unreliable in matters of money is unreliable in everything else besides."

This too, is not a romantic opinion. Even so . . .

"And now there are two such men in your life which, if you don't mind my saying so . . ."

"Steady on, Mama," murmured Nettie.

"It is only a very little money, you see. Not enough for a life of idle luxury like Nettie's. I don't think that that would do for you at all. And it certainly won't redeem your husband's debts. It is for you, only for you. Nettie agrees, don't you, Nettie?"

Nettie glanced at herself in the looking glass, inclining her pretty head.

As there was really nothing further that I could say, I took out my sheets of violet ink and began to read aloud in low, dramatic tones:

> And so, when at last he had told her that he loved only her, his delectable Maude, and had always loved her, from the moment in which he had first touched her hand in the wild garden of gloomy Nethercott Hall, then he took her in his arms and kissed her lips. She smelled the scent of his cigars, she felt neither languor nor faintness but a certain sweet fire within.
>
> "And so all that time . . ."
>
> "All that time. How could you have doubted me? I shall show you. You will not doubt me then, my dearest Maude . . ."

I did not continue. Mrs. Seawright's eyes were closing. Nettie held her hand. It had been very tricky, translating Sir Piers from a villain into a hero, but I could tell from Nettie's enraptured face that I had perhaps just managed it. It was the kisses of course, and the sweet fire within, which did it in the end, I think.

"I expect that it is the time," murmured Mrs. Seawright, "which goes to make the love. You're in it for the duration, rather like war, don't you agree?"

*

There are other sentiments, quite contrary ones too. I have even heard it said that love resembles the making of mayonnaise, that either it kicks off splendidly or else it falters from the very beginning, the vital ingredients never managing to combine quite as they should.

Last night, as it happens, Sam took me to the opera. We went to see *Prince Igor*. I do not know who it was who was meant to accompany him. He did not tell me. He simply telephoned at six o'clock, saying only, "Come to the opera with me." And when I asked, "When?" he said, "Now, Penelope. And please don't change."

I am very tin-eared, but in the course of the opera there came a melody which once upon a time my mother used to sing to me: *Take My Hand, I'm a Stranger in Paradise*.

Going out into the wet street, stepping into an old-fashioned black taxi, I hummed this tune, so sweet and haunting. It was an evening when the streets were glistening and full, delicious smells drifting from the open doorways of small, candle-lit restaurants, an evening when you do not think of the homeless, chilled people huddling nearby.

In the elevator, taking Sam home in order to grind him some very black coffee, we encountered Mrs. Munns. I remembered the occasion on which Marcus and I had met her. She was wearing her old silk evening coat, the one with the enormous round buttons and flapping cur-vaceous lapels. It's odd how bits of people, fashions too, get left over from the past, persisting into the present with such amazing obstinacy.

"Good evening, Penelope. How do you do?"

"Very well, thank you. Is it true that you are leaving soon? I shall be sad without you."

"Nobody to water your geraniums for you," said Mrs. Munns grumpily.

"That's not all there is to it, you know."

"I've discovered a stone cottage," said Mrs. Munns,

"Quite a respectable distance from my daughter's house, I think. I shall get another cat, I've always fancied a Burmese."

"You said that you were going to live with Susanna."

"Thought better of the idea. Couldn't help remembering that I dislike my sons-in-law. They are both accountants, you know. Bill taught Latin to little boys."

There was no mistaking the fact that Mrs. Munns was regarding Sam with sympathy, nothing like the evil glint which she had once visited upon poor Marcus. I decided to assuage her curiosity. It was not as if she was forever meeting me in the elevator with strange men. I don't often bring them to my flat, after all. I don't much like the way in which they pluck my books from the shelves, criticize my cooking and leave the lavatory seat up. I've always preferred civilized men.

I said, "Dear Mrs. Munns. This is my former husband. He will not be staying long."

I have never said ex-husband. It sounds horrid. Usually I just call him by his name.

"What a pity," said Mrs. Munns. "He looks rather nice. Kind too. That's not as common as you'd think."

Generally Sam does not admire the way in which ladies like Mrs. Munns dissect people's qualities to their very faces. Tonight though, he did not appear to mind at all.

"I've known worse," I replied. "We just didn't get on, that's the thing. We never saw eye to eye. We argued a great deal."

It was perfectly plain that, left to their own devices, the two of them would have got on famously. They might have had an agreeable chat about classical matters or perhaps even the shocking neglect with which I treat my poor frail geraniums. By now Sam was pressing buttons, delighting in my embarrassment. They had even begun a conversation about cats.

"A Burmese can be very temperamental. There's a

great deal to be said for a healthy, grateful, stray cat. Much more companionable."

Mrs. Munns nodded, turned pink, began to unbutton the round buttons of her ancient evening coat.

"Perhaps you are right. It was only an idea. I thought that after Reginald . . ."

"Reginald was a black cat, wasn't he? I'd have a nice marmalade one if I were you. A female, perhaps."

The elevator bumped to its bone-shattering halt. The door opened, Sam stood aside for Mrs. Munns. He's a stickler for matters of this sort, in an unobtrusive way. Mrs. Munns rattled her shabby evening bag, dug out a handful of enormous keys.

"I don't believe in divorce," she commented. "One man's just as troublesome as another in my opinion. As long as you don't choose an out-and-out rotter, that is. And it's the first twenty years that are the worst anyway, don't you think so?"

*

Wednesday, at half-past ten.

As I have written, the news of Mrs. Seawright's death came to me in the early morning, just as I was drinking my lemon tea.

After a little while, I began to picture Mrs. Seawright proclaiming the lines from her volume of *Ilios* and pouring golden brandy from her glittering decanter. I thought of her seated upright upon the cinnamon-coloured sofa at Marseilles, beneath the glass dome of the Hotel Oriental, attempting to persuade Nettie to swallow just a single mouthful of bread.

I have not grown used to people dying. I wish that they would stop. Rupert has told me that this is nothing but a childish whim and that it is time that I grew up. But there

Rupert is quite wrong. It is children who bear death with equanimity, not grown-up people at all.

*

It was three o'clock in the morning before I got on to Edith Piaf or Buddy Holly. By that time my blue-painted flat had grown icy and there was a brown nineteenth-century London mist lapping the stiff dead hydrangea bushes in the garden below. I did not bother to turn on the boiler or fetch a pair of woolly kneesocks from my chest of drawers because the insinuating November damp rather accorded with my own grim humour.

As I have written, I'm tin-eared when it comes to music. It's the words that I like the best. I can quite understand how Adelina fell for Mr. Nicolopulo, always buttering her up in that silky voice of his. It's what we all long for, after all.

*

Wednesday afternoon.

Went with Dickie to the Sweet Waters of Europe where we promenaded fashionably. The Sweet Waters are very famous, Mr. N. devoted pages to them in his book. I occupied my time in telling Dickie about my final call upon Mrs. Seawright. Dickie said that he only thinks of death in the very middle of the night and that whenever he does he is seized by a violent pounding within his chest and a fierce tightening of his throat. It only grows better, he says, when boiling tears begin to course down his cheeks.

I said that to me these sensations sounded very like panic. At which Dickie only laughed, saying, "And so they are, Addie. Unalloyed panic. You've got it exactly."

202

But upon my return to my chamber, my newly-found sympathy for Rupert vanished in a puff of smoke. He has done what I can never forgive. He has read my journal. He has not simply read it – he has <u>rifled</u> it. The pages are creased and grubby, as though it had maddened him simply to touch them. He has even gone so far as to compose an entry of his own and leave it behind on my rosewood table. I am thankful that he did not find a single word of poor Maude's story, that being securely locked in my writing box. Here is what he had the temerity to write:

> My Dear,
> You have been so very strange lately that I have taken the liberty of investigating you further, in short, I have read your journal. I am injured by it, Addie – what you said about the husband of the diarist remaining a shadowy figure. Well. I don't think that I would have minded so much if I had been nothing but a shadowy figure. But really. I'm not the shadowy figure in your diary. I am the villain. And I do mind that. I mind a very great deal. And then, everything is told from your own point of view. How do you justify that? And what's all this about Mr. Nicolopulo? Of course he was an oily stinker, Addie. He was after you and then he got cold feet. It's a common complaint, found in a great many places – not simply within your family. If you understood the world better, you would know that. When we return to London I shall take you to a doctor. I shall consult your Papa. Perhaps Sheringham might have been better than Constantinople after all. And as for the story of Madame C. – there isn't a word of truth in it. Not a word. You have such a lurid, jealous imagination. Just show me this famous pearl stud, Addie. I defy you.

But did he really expect me to write my diary from <u>his</u> point of view? How very astonishing. I never knew.

203

And that's when I realized that he had even gone so far as to steal the pearl stud as well, simply in order to make his own story seem the better of the two.

*

My very last journey to Cambridge. How comforting to know that Adelina survived this little bit of downside, flourished for fifty years more, grew rich and married Walter Ramage. Perhaps that should be consolation for the rest of us. I do hope so. Today is November the 8th and by this time next week Professor Mackintosh's house will no longer belong to me. It will belong to strange people who intend to rebuild the conservatory in the style to which it is accustomed. They have been purchasing Doulton pots and antique chairs of celebrated ironwork, all to be painted white. The old tiles, honey-coloured and maroon, are to be prised from the earth. Fresh new ones are to be laid in their place. But what on earth will they do with the elm-seated china lavatories, so authentic but so very unhygienic?

This time I did not catch the train but instead I drove, through Mill Hill and Hertfordshire, Baldock and Royston. I waited patiently for little empty blue trains with only two carriages to cross my path. I remembered the journeys of the past: Adelina journeying with Mademoiselle Aimée, drinking tea with Uncle Edgar at the Great Eastern Hotel; my father journeying on top of a crate of oranges; journeys with my mother in her shiny black old Morris; journeys with Sam; journeys hitch-hiking; journeys of all sorts, only the destination ever the same.

At Baldock, as I turned the corner beside the George and Dragon, I remembered that I had never visited Adelina's grave, did not even know how old she was at the time of her journey to Constantinople. Not as old as I am now, I am certain of that.

As I unlocked the front door of the house, the stained glass fanlight rattling in its frame, I thought that I could hear the sound of the voices of the past – mousseux-flavoured Dickie, port-flavoured Adelina, the rich, deep, gloomy Chopinesque tones of my father, not to mention the voice of my own mother, brisk and crisp and jolly hockey sticks. Outmoded voices, every one. The accents of the past.

As I opened the door and stepped into the tiled hall, treading over free newspapers, charitable envelopes and generous offers of loans of all sorts, I heard their voices retreating, dying away, as if I had come for the sole purpose of interrupting their conversation, spoiling their soirée.

"Is there anybody there?" I shouted grimly.

But of course there wasn't. No-one at all. Not if you did not count spiders.

I began rummaging through the pages of my address book, searching for the telephone number of the people who were about to buy my house.

*

The next morning.

Several hours passed in which I lay on my bed. It was very warm, the air outside my window was full of insects, buzzing and carousing. In the early light of the morning, Rupert entered.

I think that I caught a note of despair in the way in which one shoe at a time went tumbling on to the floor, thud, thud, a sound which was filled with the beat of doom. But perhaps I only imagined this, inferring what was never present, lending significance where there was none to be found. It is a habit of mine, after all.

In order to grow cooler, I fashioned a winter afternoon,

with tea and golden toasted bread, skating, ginger wine, a dagger sharp wind blowing from the north, Siberian gusty. I pulled the satin eiderdown even higher. I saw sleet, brown puddles, thin black cats shivering on the garden wall, little balls of ice striking the green glass of my father's conservatory. Such stories of cold soothed and refreshed me.

Outside my window, the insects vanished as a soft salubrious rain began to fall. It pattered away, rinsing the steps of the terrace, the white ironwork tea tables, the scented and dusty roses.

I shall book passage on the Orient Express; I shall visit Sofia and Belgrade. Tomorrow – is tomorrow Friday? – I shall attend the Friday prayers with Mr. Murat Bey. You never know what will occur next, that is the very best thing to be observed about being alive.

In my dreams, a man with black hair wandered in a still garden. It was winter, the lilac was naked. There was not a breath of bird song. The ground was frost-bitten, it cracked beneath his feet. He did not look at me but turned away, as Sir Piers Vicary might have done. He took a cigar from a silver case, sniffed it, lit it.

*

I told them that there was another house for sale in the very next street, just as nice too.

"And with a brand new roof as well. My roof leaks, you know. The rain seeps in. You have to arrange tin buckets in the attic. It's very inconvenient. My estate agent said cruel things about the house when I first decided to sell it."

"You can't do this to us. It's monstrous."

"It isn't kind, I know. Just the same . . ."

At first I felt a little rush of guilt between my shoulder blades. After that, nothing at all. The house is mine. How foolish to think that I might abandon it so easily.

"I imagine you're waiting for us to cough up more money, aren't you?"

"No, oh no. I'm very sorry. I have changed my mind, you see."

A change of heart, I thought. That is how I shall describe it. Everyone will understand.

Now that business is not transacted quite as furiously as it once was, the estate agent who so charmed Victoria is mellow and sweet-tempered.

"How lovely to hear from you. How are you? No flu? I do hope not."

I said, "I shall not sell my house, I've had a change of heart."

But the words did not soothe him as I had hoped.

"Am I to understand . . . Are you telling me that . . . You should take a little while to consider, you know . . . Perhaps . . ." he blithered into the telephone.

*

Friday. I do not know what date it is.

It occurred to me, some time yesterday, that I would change Maude Arabella's name to Esther, Esther Louisa, I think. But Esther Louisa what? Maude is a silly name, a silly girl in a silly poem, and Arabella is far too frivolous a name for anyone sensible to possess. My father was never enchanted by Tennyson. Kitty was the one who read Tennyson. Mademoiselle Aimée only agreed with French poems, some very peculiar stuff too. Rupert never agreed with poetry at all. So, Esther. But Sir Piers Vicary will remain Sir Piers and . . .

*

But she did not change Maude Arabella's name. Nowadays, it is naturally far easier to effect such wholesale amendments. Then it was more difficult. In *The Lady From The Seraglio*, Maude remains Maude. That's the sort of detail I can be relied on to know about.

I am on my way to visit another bookshop. The proprietor has found something to my advantage, a celebrated dragoman's guide to Constantinople.

*

Friday Continued.

I shall not describe the palace (kiosk is, I think, the proper name for it) at Yildiz. Mr. N.'s account, drab and flavourless as it is, must do.

The road was rutted, wild and dusty. We travelled in a closed fiacre, swaying madly to and fro, so that, from time to time, Murat Bey was obliged to take my arm or grip my shoulders, holding me tightly against his body – which, I must say, was neither plump and well-fed as Mr Nicolopulo's, nor chilly and perfunctory as Rupert's is. I shall not describe the sensation which this gave me for that would, I fear, require violet ink.

Everyone travels to Yildiz by this most unsatisfactory road – diplomats, visiting emperors, curious foreign ladies and glittering Turkish officers. In front of us, ensconced in an open landau, there travelled the wife of a newly accredited ambassador, a tall and disdainful lady who grew distraught as the clouds of stinking dust enveloped her. We rumbled by little knots of disconsolate and ragged beggars, the sellers of sweetmeats, poor pitiful children and roaming bands of Mrs. Elliot's famous pariah dogs.

Silenced by this spectacle of life, Mr. Murat Bey (for that is how I think of him) covered his eyes with his hands. His hands are the hands of a violin player – long and pale and supple. It is the one thing in which he resembles Mr. N. – this shame at the state of his country.

He gave a French shrug, wonderfully hopeless.

"What will happen here?"

"Anything at all. There is no telling."

I have written that the Sultan passes his days in solitude, never visiting Stamboul or journeying abroad. I have not written that he does not even walk in his park or fish the waters of the Bosphorus. He is unknown to his people, few of whom would recognize him if they stumbled into him in the spice bazaar.

"The Sultan might be murdered, the Empire might fall to pieces. It has already begun to crumble and crack. There might be reform. It is not impossible."

I could tell that although he had sympathy for this last hope, still he did not think that it would happen soon. A grim frown visited his face. He drew down a white tasselled blind so that I might no longer look out upon the streets.

"Please do not."

And then he explained to me that my enchantment with Turkey was owing to the circumstances of my ordered girlhood, my own ordered nation. I was enchanted, he said, because for persons of my sort, a visit to Stamboul was a joyful escape from the patterns and procedures of my own calm life.

A slight coldness then ensued, broken only by our arrival at Yildiz. There everything was entirely ordered and determined. The ambassadress who had preceded us vanished into a secret diplomatic chamber. Albanian officers in their brilliantly embroidered coats smiled invitingly at the prettier of the foreign ladies. Tea and coffee were brought while everyone preened themselves, it being the case that only foreigners with distinguished introductions may come to glimpse the Sultan. My companion began to tell stories of the wives of his grandfather, a

209

Circassian among them, and how they had schemed and plotted to defeat the old man at every turn, baulking all of his dearest wishes and turning him into a pitiable invalid.

"It's all very well for a strong and healthy man to possess four wives. It's quite another matter for someone rickety and fragile."

"Mmm, I dare say."

I was astonished by my first sight of the Sultan. His face was white, hollow. He stooped, a small round-shouldered man. He glanced neither to the left nor to the right, as if perhaps he did not know that we had come simply in order to observe him as though he were nothing but a mangy, pacing lion at the London zoo.

"There he is," said Murat Bey. "A man who is consumed with fear. He is afraid of underhanded poisons, sudden bullets, Nihilist bombs . . ."

Nihilist bombs, fair-haired Russian ladies with a predilection for tea and ideology, il n'y a que mystère et roman. Had I lived in the eighteenth century, there is no doubt that I would have been an associationist.

*

I must confess that I had longed for something rather more racy and exciting than that which is to follow. I had imagined that there might be pages of violet ink, that perhaps Rupert might catch her – in flagrante, as was once said, full-length upon her silken chaise longue. But instead it appears that it is Mademoiselle Aimée's counsel which has prevailed at the last and that the most diverting things of all have been left out.

Another difference between life and books: in books you must expect drama; in life you must expect secrets.

*

After the Selamlik.

Our return journey was exceedingly quick, as return journeys so often are. In the fiacre, Murat Bey looked questioningly into my face.

"Do you remember the harbour at Marseilles?"

"I do, yes."

"And how you first saw me?"

Whether to lie? Undoubtedly. But . . .

"Yes, I remember that too."

He nodded, as if that were all that he required to know.

When we had arrived at The Summer Palace Hotel, he took my elbow. "Shall we have tea? Perhaps in your sitting-room?"

"Yes, that is what I would like."

But the tea of course came afterwards. On our way he lit a cigarette, the smoke drifted down the long corridor where once I had run in the middle of the night, silver slippers on my feet, just like Maude Arabella.

I did not expect to suffer diabolical faintness.

*

I would like to end by composing a disquisition on the subject of these ubiquitous cigarettes. How once they were considered wicked and intoxicating but how nowadays, they are regarded as perfectly disgusting. How once they were symbolic of a dashing female emancipation but how nowadays, the smoking of a cigarette is taken to indicate addiction and enslavement of the most unrepentantly depraved variety. Instead though, I shall write an account of Mr. Nicolopulo's book, and how I found it in a secondhand bookshop not far away from Auntie's Tea Room and St. Mary's Church.

The proprietor of the bookshop, a man by the name of Mr. Giles, had mournful watery eyes and a yellow

211

submariner's beard. The shop was so icy that he had balanced a woolly hat on the pinnacle of his head. He was embroiled in the report of a cricketing correspondent, composed in some balmy and faraway place. On one wall, there was a decorative collection of Harmsworth's *History of the World*; at the other end of the shelf were green cloth volumes of Trollope. Fact seeping into fiction, as is so often the case.

He handed me a copy of *A Celebrated Dragoman's Unerring Companion to Constantinople*.

I explained that I had doubted the very existence of its author and that I was rather glad to find that he had really lived after all.

"So you thought this Nicolopulo chap didn't exist?"

"Mmm, well, something along those lines. You see . . ."

"And would it matter if he didn't?"

"Yes, yes I think so. You have to be able to tell the difference between what's made up and what isn't, you know."

"D'you mind if I . . . ?"

"Of course not. It's your shop, after all."

A cloud of cheap, thin, grey smoke filled the air, not in the least like Mrs. Seawright's thoughtful blue smoke or Murat Bey's alluring seductive smoke. It was modern smoke. Mountains of it rose in the air, Harmsworth and Trollope vanished.

"The bank's," he said sorrowfully, throwing away a match. "Not mine at all."

"Ah."

"Actually, I specialize in Arctic adventures. I've got a very nice copy of *The Worst Journey In The World*. Apsley Cherry Gerrard, you know. Books of that sort are only required in the summertime. Would you like to see it?"

It was the right sort of day for it, little tight balls of hail colliding with the pavement outside, a blistering salty wind. And in any case I was a little undecided as to where to go next.

"Yes, please."

His movements grew a little more brisk at the thought of selling two books instead of one. The cloud of grey smoke enveloped him as he stepped away. I began turning the pages of Mr. Nicolopulo's book, sniffing them, searching them for bookmarks and brown unscented desiccated flowers. I discovered the description of the palace at Yildiz, it's not exactly as Adelina records it. There's a word changed, here and there – and for the better too, I think.

It's not simply the resounding of the words in my head which I've always loved about books, it is the things themselves, the very thingness of them. The astonishing way in which they fit into your hands; the very texture of their covers – occasionally limp, occasionally stern. Their agreeably tantalizing paper wrappers.

"Did you ever hear of Adelina Mackintosh? She wrote travel books too, you know. Not polar journeys though, not entirely your cup of tea."

"Got one here," he said. "Romania and Bulgaria, written some time after the Russo-Turkish war. One of those hideous nineteenth-century females, you know, shelving bosoms and hair brooches, hardly human at all. Best thing about the Somme, in my opinion. It put a stop to people like her."

"Mmm," I said, as he put the fat old book into my hands.

And there it was. The building of Sofia, all contracts and corrupt officials, and Turno-Severin, where my grandmother was born – a dusty, backward, provincial town, a stopping place for the railway. The sort of place where bored and forgotten officers fought fearsome duels. It was very bizarre, the way in which the prose resembled Mariora Silver's but had been put to such a very different purpose.

I began to read a passage aloud but I stopped pretty quickly when I saw the expression on his face.

"I shall have this too. May I write a cheque?" I asked politely.

"I wish you would," he smiled gravely.

I rummaged for my cheque book, wrote my name. He tied my books in an old-fashioned brown paper parcel. I think that he was eager to return to his newspaper article. He had begun huffing and puffing and combing his fingers through his submariner's beard.

"I must get a gas fire," he mumbled. "Talk about brass monkeys."

I think that Marcus and Julia would be astounded to learn that some people still have little gas fires, coin in the slot gas metres too.

"I expect that you read a great many books, don't you?"

"Certainly not," replied Mr. Giles, picking up his newspaper. "I wouldn't know where to begin, would I?"

*

Tea-time.

"Are you feeling sadly?" enquired Murat Bey, just as I was deciding that I would not allow myself to fall in love with him all over again.

"Oh no," I replied. "The very opposite."

I was still impaled upon my chaise longue, the sighing and murmuring just over.

"That is because I have brought you pleasure," he declared.

"I think that must be true."

But I am afraid that I was already thinking of Maude Arabella and the ending of her story. How might I indicate that . . . Perhaps a train journey to Scotland, a tunnel. I would be obliged to move Nethercott Hall, Sir Piers's gloomy estate. I would make it a castle instead. A castle on an icy western headland, a <u>moated</u> castle, the survivor of fierce sieges.

214

"And you have been delightfully useful too."

This news did not disturb him, as I was afraid it might. The very opposite.

"Have I? And what are you thinking of now?"

"Of a postcard which I must write, and . . ."

I was thinking of Walter, as a matter of fact — picturing him upon the chaise longue. He would not go in for impaling but would favour a gentler course, I do believe.

*

In the end I journeyed north, along the narrow straightness of the A 10, in the direction of the Wash and the Norfolk coast.

As I drove, the watery light began vanishing into the west. It was natural to imagine that Adelina was travelling with me. I was undecided as to whether I should conjure her as the Floris-scented old lady whom I had once known or whether to picture her wearing a bustle, a hobble skirt or a drop-waisted frock from the twenties. I began to consider my biography, how I could pack Adelina's bags, drive her to the station, put her on the Orient Express, turn the wheels of her train in the direction of Belgrade, the Iron Gate, Vienna. I could write of the Balkans and how they were changing in those years, of how Sofia was a city surrounded by mountains, thronging with strangers, Jews, Greeks and Frenchmen. I might discover what happened to Murat Bey in the remainder of his life, how he captured bandits in the province of Smyrna and perhaps survived in order to become a plump and accomplished official in the modern Turkey.

Naturally, the events in Turno-Severin, the birth of my grandmother, would be difficult to describe. There were no witnesses, no letters remaining to be found in mysterious, obliging attics and I did not want to write "Adelina must indeed have supposed" or "It was perhaps on a steamy July day that . . .". There are occasions, after all, when you can discover no more. If you feel tempted, then you may embroider the emptiness with make-believe, if not, then not.

*

My Dear Papa,
Do you see the whirling dervish? I do hope so. Tomorrow Rupert will take me to the station. You must send my love to everyone I know. I shall be travelling in the Balkans for the next few months. I am going with a lady called Madame Chrissavelonis, her little girls are going too. You must not worry. Madame C. is the soul of respectability. Do not think of me if you can help it. I have changed, you see, and you may not like me quite as I am at the moment. Please remember me to Walter if he should call to argue with you.

That is not precisely what I would like to tell Papa. Just the same, it will have to do for the time being. As for Rupert, he turned quite white when I said that I was leaving. He reminded me of my duties.

"You shan't have a penny more," he spluttered.

"I am making a visit to Sofia with Madame Chrissavelonis. I shall leave in the morning after Mrs. Seawright's funeral. You will hear from me very soon, Rupert."

"Not a penny. I mean it."

"I shan't require one."

He was thunderstruck. He began rummaging his fingers through his hair, scratching his wrists.

"I have bought some new studs for you. They came from the bazaar. I hope you don't lose them quite so often as the others."

"Shall we send for some wine?" he enquired soothingly. "Perhaps we should discuss the matter. I'm not entirely certain that this is all my fault."

216

But as everybody agrees, there are moments when discussion is to no purpose whatsoever, moments when it becomes crystally clear that it no longer matters whose fault it is, moments when you realize that you have been having the same discussion for years and years on end and that there is absolutely no remedy to be found.

*

Mmm, well, there are definitely moments when one feels like that. Nevertheless . . .

I drew the car to a stop outside the red telephone box in the village in Fincham. I tugged fiercely at the hand brake. Fincham has a great deal in common with Mrs. Munns's evening coat: it belongs in the past and persists into the present. It has a pub, a church of simple perpendicular gravity and, of course, a red telephone box.

I dialled the number of the fisherman's cottage in Wells. No-one answered. In the distance the bell of the telephone pealed. It was an indignant, constant sort of peal. I imagined Antigone, rolling upon the plain white gas boiler, her warm-blooded ears standing to attention. A shadow of a question flitted across my mind: who can write of cats with the affection and precision of Colette? Answer: nobody at all.

I rammed the phone back into its horrid cradle. Even in Fincham the telephone booth smells, I am ashamed to record.

But what should I do next?

I drove on.

*

September, 1894. Between Stamboul and Sofia.

My Dear Kitty,

I might write pages and pages, armies of words, but you would still be vexed and saddened by what I have done. But

217

if I carry on as I am, Kitty, then nobody will ever remember me and I have such a passion to be remembered. I know that you do not have such selfish and vulgar thoughts, dear Kitty. Please forgive me.

Another thing – please ask your kind husband, Mr. Alston, to advise poor Rupert. I am afraid that his affairs are in a horrid muddle and there is no speck of hope that he will take my advice.

I remain your loving friend,
Adelina

*

It was quite black by the time that I got to Wells. There was no longer any hail falling but only a gently chilly rain blown in from the North Sea. The windows of the town were steamy, there was a glow from the interior of the ship chandlery. It was the sort of night on which a person can feel quite bereft if only they put their minds to it. In between the bursts of pattering rain, the windscreen wipers made sticky, squeaking noises.

I abandoned the car down on the front, buttoned my raincoat and began to splash through the puddles.

In Sam's little house the lights were on. On the ledge of the sitting-room window there sat a grumpy, glossy cat. I did not speak to the cat for it is a well-known fact that cats have no sympathy with those who simply want to curry favour.

When he had opened the door, Sam took me in his arms.

How lovely, I thought. How unexpected. How I have missed this. I thought it would all be more complicated.

"Who said that happiness was only to be found at the end of an English novel?" enquired Sam.

I considered for a moment. It's sad that I cannot remember things quite as plainly as I once did.

"Wicked, beautiful Madame Neroni," I replied. "The one who makes mincemeat of Mr. Slope."

I did not feel inclined to say *poor* Mr. Slope.

"In *Barchester Towers*," I added.

"Mmm," laughed Sam. "Who could forget Madame Neroni, even at a moment like this?"

And that is exactly where we see eye to eye.